About the Author

Robert Crane started writing seriously during one of his backpacking trips. He honed his storytelling skills as an English teacher. He has published articles, poems, and essays in small journals. Robert, an American, has been living in Oslo, Norway, for the past twenty years.

Take a Look at Me Now

Robert P Crane

Take a Look at Me Now

Olympia Publishers
London

www.olympiapublishers.com
OLYMPIA PAPERBACK EDITION

Copyright © Robert P Crane 2024

The right of Robert P Crane to be identified as author of
this work has been asserted in accordance with sections 77 and 78 of
the Copyright, Designs and Patents Act 1988.

All Rights Reserved

No reproduction, copy or transmission of this publication
may be made without written permission.
No paragraph of this publication may be reproduced,
copied or transmitted save with the written permission of the publisher,
or in accordance with the provisions
of the Copyright Act 1956 (as amended).

Any person who commits any unauthorised act in relation to
this publication may be liable to criminal
prosecution and civil claims for damage.

A CIP catalogue record for this title is
available from the British Library.

ISBN: 978-1-80439-899-9

This is a work of fiction.
Names, characters, places and incidents originate from the writer's
imagination. Any resemblance to actual persons, living or dead, is
purely coincidental.

First Published in 2024

Olympia Publishers
Tallis House
2 Tallis Street
London
EC4Y 0AB

Printed in Great Britain

Dedication

This book is dedicated to the memory of my mother, Barbara Crane.

"Men don't begin to live fully until their backs are against the wall."
　　– Francois-Rene de Chateaubriand

Part 1 – Wallowing

Chapter 1

Bubby Welter, fifteen, sat on the couch under the gaze of the TV. His mother was in the dining room shuffling papers, bank statements, around on the table. The plant on the windowsill had died of thirst. Yellow spots on the green leaves. Bubby glimpsed her bent over, cigarette smoke curling up into the air.

The money dropped into her purse from her dead father, Jess Bagley. They had sat in the funeral parlor; Carrie Welter wept through her speech. Bubby's necktie choked him. He hardly knew the guy. They stood by the grave as the dirt was thrown on top of the casket. His mother erupted. Bubby just sat and stared at the cars, wondering at makes and models. He couldn't understand why she was being so melodramatic. Didn't she complain to him about her father? He wondered what the man looked like now in the box underneath all the dirt.

Bubby didn't dare ask her how much. They were supposed to move to a house in the suburbs, but Carrie Welter couldn't get started. But she enjoyed going to the machine and pulling stacks from the slot. There she was one day waving a card hand of '20s in Bubby's direction. He stared at the fan, afraid to reach out for one of the bills. Then she pulled them back and put them behind her. Bubby said oh well in his mind. She did it again. This time he reached for a bill. When he did, she tightened her grasp. She arranged them in a stack, stamped it on the table, and sheepishly handed over a bill to her son.

He looked at it crooked and waited for her to snatch it back.

"Go on and take it." She gave him five choices on what he could do with it, then wrote off each one when he picked up the bill. Go and buy something. Not this, not that, though.

Carrie groaned now. She lifted herself off the chair and trudged into the kitchen. Bubby heard her opening cabinets, cursing. Then the uncapping of a pill bottle, the water running, the pill going down the gullet. Bubby stared at the set. Diving into the images shooting from the screen, trying to focus on the voices of the actors, lumpish, mesmerized.

Carrie put her hands in the back pockets of her jeans and stared. Her eyes were drained of color. Bubby looked over at her, curious as to how far the pill she had swallowed had wormed its way through her innards. He went to another show. The words and images were all familiar to him. His mother was about to exclaim, "Let's get out of here, Bub. What do you say?" She didn't though. She went back to the bank statements. Bubby heard her cursing from the other room. He wanted to know the figure. How many digits? She was back in the living room. Bubby couldn't look at her. He became one with the drone of the TV while he slowly tapped the remote against his thigh. "Things are going to change, Bubby."

"Mmm, *hmm*."

"Come on, Bub, show some enthusiasm."

"Mmm, okay."

Bubby looked over at his mother who was scratching maniacally at her scalp. The other held a cigarette. She'd shout at him or raise her hand. The buxom actress did it to him. He'd get up and excuse himself, retreat to his room, where he'd be free to explore and disperse. The problem was, he lacked the energy and wherewithal to climb off the couch.

"I'm not saying we're on easy street," Carrie was saying.

"But we're close." She burst into laughter.

Bubby laughed along for a bit, then stopped. She carried on. Bubby sat there in a ring of her cackles. "Let's go and get you some new duds, *hmm*?" Bubby was still thinking about running for the shelter of his room.

"It's the duds that make the man."

His mother laughed at her own comment. Bubby tried not to lock eyes with her.

"Get out of your tracksuit and put on something else." It took Bubby much longer than it should have for him to lift himself off the sofa.

"Come on, Bub. Move it." He was finally on his feet. "That's it. There you go. Right on."

Bubby muttered under his breath, "Mom, please." She stood in the doorway of his room which was in tatters. Clothes strewn everywhere, papers – old homework assignments, no doubt – heaped on the desk. Bubby picked out a shirt and a pair of pants. Carrie was gone. Bubby put the clothes on his bed and smelled his pits.

Then Mother was back. "No," she said. "That won't do," she was holding a packet; skimming through the pages. Bubby froze in the middle of the room. "Look at this house. Out in the suburbs. It's totally within our range." Carrie stared from page to nothing at all. Bubby was throwing the shirt and pants into the closet.

He held another shirt and pair of pants up to his mother. "Yeah, yes. That's good, Bub." Bubby held the pants and waited for his mother to leave the room. "Of course, you'll have to start up at a new school, and what with all the upkeep on the house. I remember your grandfather complaining about it all the time. 'Damn hedges, stupid lawn. They just keep on growing. It's a menace.' Let's weigh our options." Bubby was waiting. "No, Bubby. That doesn't match."

Bubby looked at her, then away. A strange tickle in his feet. It grew in intensity and then started climbing up his legs, until it jammed his heart and stopped his blood from flowing. "What about these?" He held up a blue shirt and black pants. He turned to find a gap where his mother just stood. He got the shirt over his pudge. The pants were harder to get on. He put each foot through the legs, then sat on the bed to finish the job. It cost him strength and offered up frustration. He was panting. The belt was hard to get on. Too many loops, not enough holes. She was back. "No, no." She would break down and cry. Bubby was about to get the belt buckled. He looked at her and saw glass about to shatter. Or a volcano about to erupt.

"Mom?"

"Go with the first outfit." She was thumbing through the pages again. "Interest rates are on our side. We can surely find something out there. You and me, Bubs. What do you say?"

"I..."

"When we get back, this room needs to be picked up."

"Mom..."

She couldn't answer because she had left the room.

The store was packed. For the boy, it was a slog. His mother led the charge, even though she couldn't pick a direction. They wove and wended their way through the crowds. Bubby fell into a cave in the boy's department. Carrie began picking out shirts, pants, jackets, holding them up to her befuddled son. Bubby felt his way through the confusion.

"What do you want, Bubs?" She held the brown shirt up to his chest.

"I don't know," he muttered. Bubby watched another mother and son combo across the way. It was a pair from one of his TV shows. Soon she would utter the words, "Isn't this grand? Isn't life peachy?"

"We'll take this shirt and these pants. Yes, Bubs, they suit you. It's what you want, right?" She didn't wait for him to respond, nor did she care. Bubby had scenarios from situational comedies running through his head. Pretty soon he'd be stranded on his own island, starving and thirsting, if he didn't get back to his TV set. Carrie was fuming. She couldn't make up her mind. She held three shirts up at once, pushing them one by one to Bubby's chest. That anger turned to rage. Bubby could spill out of himself. He wanted to run through the store upsetting all the items of clothing.

"Just pick." His words were sludge. He didn't care at all which clothes he walked out of the store with. Carrie deposited the heap on the rack and stormed off. Bubby was awash in bliss. He watched his mother scamper through the far end of the boy's department. The ceiling could collapse, and Bubby would still be floundering in joy. *She'll run away*, he thought. *I'll get the debit card. I'll have carte blanche and a TV in my room.*

She was back, though, once again sporting an armload of clothes. "This jacket is perfect for you."

"Let's get it. Get all of it."

"Bubby!"

"No. We'll get the other shirt. These things don't suit you."

"Whatever." The anger spread through his chest. He wondered if the inheritance was doing anything positive for her. Could the money be rotten?

Carrie tore off. Bubby halted. He looked around the store. Someone from school was here. Any other boy he knew in the same predicament? He found his mother on a bench. She had her head in her hands. Bubby studied her. She was crying. He took a step toward her. There was nothing he could do. Then she got up and stared at her son.

"Since you don't show any interest in this, we'll just leave without buying anything."

"Fine."

"So, that's how it's going to be?"

"I guess," he spurted.

She got up and dropped all the clothes she would have bought on the bench. Then she weeded through the items and brought a jacket, shirt, and a pair of pants up to the cashier. After she paid for the clothes, Bubby had to hurry to keep pace with her as she hurtled her body out of the store.

In the line at the food court, Bubby's thoughts wheeled and whirled

Just as they had made their way to the front of the line, Carrie changed tack, grabbed her son's arm, and pulled him toward the next restaurant to the left. Bubby didn't protest. They stared up at the board. "You'll have a hoagie. And I'll have a piece of pizza." Bubby didn't want a hoagie. He wanted a piece of pizza too. He didn't make his wishes known to his mother. There was a chance she'd go into another crying jag. She pulled some bills from her purse and pressed them toward the man at the cashier. He raised an eyebrow. Bubby unwrapped his food and took a large bite. Eating allowed him to disappear. He wouldn't have to speak. Carrie talked about the houses. Bubby looked at her sideways, then went back to the sandwich. The mayonnaise oozed onto his fingers, which he began licking and slurping up. He took another massive bite and spent a while chewing. People flooded by. Carrie lit a cigarette, took two quick puffs, then pushed the cherry end of it into her piece of pizza. It made a forlorn L shape. "Listen, Bub. The properties are glorious. The rooms splendid. Ceilings arched. Neighborhood's immaculate. You have to see the greenery. The tree-lined roads. People going hand in hand. Kids playing, safe. There's a country club, Bub. See how well kept everything is, Bubs. We're beginning again. Jumping into our future."

Bubby felt deflated when he came to the end of his hoagie. He would be expected to talk now, to contribute. How would he ever get a word in? He just wanted to be in front of the TV set. Comforted, calmed, and taken care of.

They got back to the building. Bubby had the bundle under his arm. As they entered the foyer, Mr. Swanson met them coming down the stairs. He was wearing a tweed cap and a long black coat. "Hi, Carrie."

He smiled wryly at his mother. "Hi, Bubby." The boy picked something up.

She seemed to have a train of conversational tidbits lined up in her head ready to be delivered. Mr. Swanson waited. Nothing came, so he moved toward the door, "Going to get cold now," he said, then pushed the door open and walked out.

"He is an odd one," Carrie said.

Bubby shrugged but didn't say anything. They trudged up to the third floor. Bubby dropped the bag of clothes on his bed and went and stood in front of his full-length mirror. He took off his shirt and groaned. He had love handles. At fifteen. He turned and cursed at the sight of his plump backside. He thought of all the kids at school who went to the weight room or jogged around the track, Bob Tyson, that ripped torso, and the girls who swarmed around him. The thoughts were forming. He put his tracksuit back on and went out to the living room and flopped onto his backside on the couch. The remote wasn't working. Bubby pecked at it. Nothing. He pushed harder, harder. He'd have to get up and do it the old-fashioned way. What an inconvenience. He lay and listened to his mother who was in the kitchen. Bubby sighed, then made his way to the dining room in search of batteries.

He could see his mother from there. She was weeping. Bubby stood there and watched and listened. She had a pill bottle next to where she stood. Bubby gathered some soothing words he'd heard said on one of his shows. He had it all formed in his head. "You'll pull through. There's a calm after the storm."

He just stood there. No words left his mouth. Carrie opened the bottle of pills and removed two or three. She slammed the faucet on and filled a glass with water. She let out a whimper. The sobbing was over. Bubby was still trying to come up with the right words when his mother turned. She was startled. "Bubby. I..." She was rubbing her eyes. Bubby felt drained all of a sudden. He looked toward the living room, the place where he could find shelter.

"You'll pull out of this." He surprised himself.

"Yes, yes, Bub. Now let's have a fashion show. Try on your new duds." Bubby looked at the set. It was waiting for him. He had the batteries in his hand. "Go on." Bubby walked into his room and started getting out of the tracksuit. The chubs were still there. The new blue shirt barely concealed them. He sighed again. The pants were tight. He miraculously got them up to his waist. Then the new brown shoes. The life in him sailed away. It was all wrong and awkward. He'd stand out at school in these clothes. He went into the living room and tried to look up. "Those are nice." She stared at him. "The pants. I'm not so sure. What do you think?" Bubby didn't have a chance to respond. She talked on. "No. They won't do. Strip them off and we'll return them."

"Mom! They're fine!"

"Bubby. Watch that tone." Fifteen minutes later, the batteries were in the remote, and it was working as normal. The TV filled the room, and his head. His mother was at the kitchen table smoking and going through the packet. Bubby looked over from time to time. She could explode. Fall out the window. Cry herself to death. Drink poison. Drop down the garbage chute, slide down the disposal and get mauled, get shot by a stray bullet, disappear, just vanish in thin air. Bubby wanted to know the figure. He couldn't ask though. It had to have a lot of zeroes in it. *How to ask?* This wasn't the right time. Bubby was shot out from thinking. He stared into the set. *Cool*, he thought. *It's one I've seen before. A good one.*

Night fell. His mother had retreated to her bedroom and now Bubby could stuff his hand down his pants. He felt around, then gave up, worried that she'd come back. A new show came on. Bubby couldn't get into it. He thought about calling Abe but decided against it. He had nothing to say. Bubby flicked off the TV and listened to the sounds of cars rolling by on Que Street. A fire truck. The sirens of an ambulance possibly. Then silence, an oppressive quiet. He flicked the set back on and observed four people sitting around a table. One man, in a dark suit, was talking animatedly. The three others hung on his words. Bubby knew that what they were talking about was important, but he couldn't latch on to what was being said. He tried with all his might. It flew through his head and made him sleepy.

Later, he was in his room flipping through a comic book. There were books for school he was supposed to be reading, but he couldn't bring himself to open them. His mother's room was adjacent to his which made it easy for him to hear her weeping. It was a symphony: now heavy, now low and soft. Bubby ran his hands over his flab. He looked up at the ceiling. What words could he employ? How could he make himself get up and go in there? He was conflicted. On the one hand he was worried about his mother. On the other he found her helpless and pathetic.

 He got up and went and stood outside her door. She was sobbing now. Bubby felt an itch in his calves. He ran his hands vigorously over the skin. They still screamed for his nails. The weeping continued. *What a crossroads I find myself at. This is what makes the man.* Those were the words from the show. Or at least as close to the real ones as they could come.

 He walked into the living room and stared at the dark set. At the window now, looking down, wondering how many boys were being shot at not a mile from this apartment building. How life could end in a heartbeat. The cop shows had it wrong. The looks on the faces of the dying. Maybe the real looks were duller, less cinematic. Bubby shivered. He crept down the hall. His mother had stopped sobbing. She had the radio on and was listening to a talk show. Bubby sighed. He went into his room and flopped down onto the bed. Sleep would collide. He was fifteen. He had nothing to worry about. Not how he'd look in school the next day in his new clothes, not the sirens and the gunshots, not the house they might buy or his mother's moods. It all floated above him. He could reach up, but he wouldn't be able to touch them.

Monday morning arrived. It had nothing else to do but come. Bubby woke to a quiet apartment. He stared at the snow flurries trickling down from the lifeless sky. He took bowl, cereal box, spoon, and milk and plunked them down on the kitchen table. He'd let her sleep. He knew he wasn't supposed to do it, but he brought his breakfast food into the living room and flicked on the set. Talk shows, a man teaching people how to paint landscapes, more talk shows, cartoons that were beneath Bubby. He slurped up the cereal, a drop of milk formed on his chin. He had on the new brown shoes and the blue shirt. The pants were oldies. *I look ridiculous* formed in his head. *They're going to laugh me out of the place.* What's in store? He could fake it. The old trick of the thermometer up against the bulb.

He heard rustling from down the hall. She was groggy and about to throw a fit. "Bub!"

"Ya!"

"What did we discuss?"

Bubby stared. "I'll go to the table." He gathered all the things and went into the kitchen. He caught a glimpse of his mother's face. She looked weathered. Her eyes were bloodshot. *What to do*, he thought? He wanted the solace of the TV. He knew he wouldn't get it. School started in twenty minutes. No chance.

Abe was waiting outside his house on 27th Street. He was a smallish kid, but somehow appeared larger. He was wearing his parka. The jacket devoured him. "Hey, Bub."

"Hey, Abe." Bubby stared at his friend and then looked out into the distance where the tiny snowflakes were zigzagging down. The woman on the show had told her friend that she was only in it for herself. Bubby tried to find something to talk about with his friend. His mind went blank. They walked down 27th.

Carter High School loomed in the distance. Bubby was entering a penitentiary. He just lacked the cuffs and the orange jumpsuit.

"So, you're in Bub?" Bubby looked away from his friend. "Me, personally," Abe said. "I don't trust this Devon kid. I don't like his aura or the smell of him."

He wracked his brain. Nothing floated up. The lack of thinking began to make him nervous. Something zapped in his head. Flashes of lightning going back and forth never striking anything. He couldn't stop it.

"I'll meet him after school today but I'm not making any promises that I'll follow him into his hijinks," Abe said.

Bubby shoved his hands into his pockets. "Good and evil need each other." Abe looked at his friend. He couldn't come up with anything to say to that. Bubby wasn't sure where he'd gotten that line.

"Are you stoned, Bub?"

Bubby barfed out a laugh.

He moved through the hallways collecting perceived glances of disapproval from all the other students. His feet wriggled in his shoes. In English, he really tried to glom on to what the teacher was saying. He dreamed of shows, more shows, the drone of the set. Bromberg was going to call on him if he wasn't careful. Bubby bent his head down into his book to seek shelter. Bromberg looked his way and Bubby readied himself. Even if he hadn't read the book, he could still regurgitate something he'd heard in class on the previous Friday. Bromberg scanned the room. Bubby glanced over at Jackie Tolleson to ease the pain, her ass fitting snugly into the chair. She looked back at him with disdain, which caused Bubby to turn away.

He ate with Abe in the far corner of the lunchroom. Buried

his head in his Tater Tots. Abe was quick and with it. Bubby envied his friend for a split second. Devon passed by and then sat down at their table. Bubby got the itch on his calves again. Devon told them they'd meet at the park by Stone Creek after school. "You know," he said. "To complete the planning stage." Abe locked eyes with Devon as if to say, you'd better come up with something good, Redson. Devon knocked his fist against the table and eyed the two other boys. Bubby had to look away after a while. When Devon had gone, Abe rolled his eyes.

"What a lout," Abe said.

"Why are we meeting him, then?"

"I want to see just how much of a schmuck this kid is. I want to see him go down." Bubby watched Devon circle the cafeteria. Something arose in Bubby's mind just as fast it vanished. The train of thoughts started, but Abe put an end to it when he started talking again, now about Devon's family.

Gym. Bubby had no choice. He was in the locker room hiding in a corner. He unbuttoned his shirt as slowly as possible, then covered his torso with his hands. He was outed, searchlights were on him. They'd all pass by and call him out for his blubber. There was no way he was getting into the showers after class. He wouldn't be able to withstand the looks and the ribbing. He stared into the locker. The gym shorts he was putting on were an obnoxious yellow color. The itching started again. The ropes hanging down from the rafters were supposed to be climbed. Bubby watched Tyson go up in five seconds flat. Bubby was mortified by his flab. A broken wrist. Diarrhea. Mono. Tonsilitis. The Clap. He was up. The rope was what he would use to hang himself. Tyson watched Bubby clasp it. Bubby got two feet up. He was sweating and panting. It was even too pathetic for the others to laugh at him. Bubby dropped to the ground. He made his way shamefacedly to the corner of the gym. He spent the rest of the class avoiding the exercises he was supposed to have been doing.

He conjugated a couple of verbs on the sheet in Spanish class. Devon Redson passed him a note at one point. You're not going to chicken out now, are you, Welter, it said. *Yes,* Bubby thought, *I mean, no.*

The snow had turned into a steady, cold rain. Abe and Bubby were waiting by Stone Creek at one of the outdoor exercise stations. "He's not going to show," Abe said. "He's a creep. Let's get out of here, my mom left food." Then Bubby saw Redson coming down the hill toward them. Devon's hat bobbed on his head as the kid made his way toward Abe and Bubby. Bubby pictured it happening. He'd seen it all on the box. A triangle made by three police cars converging on them. A hail of bullets popping through his parka, then the sweet and airy taste of death on his tongue.

"Here's the deal," Devon said. "Kathy's parents aren't home until six, and Kathy Mosely isn't the sharpest tool in the workhouse…"

"… shed," Abe said.

"Whatever," Devon said. "Just listen up."

"You're a douchebag," Abe said. Bubby put his hand over his mouth to swallow the laugh. Bubby waited for more direction from Devon. He could pick Abe over Redson. An easy decision. He looked up toward the bridge that spanned the park, way up high. A TV drama. The dialogue. It ran through his head. Sharpshooters speaking in whispers up on the bridge. SWAT team in their places. Devon was talking again.

"We don't need you, then, Abraham." They all stood there looking at each other. Bubby needed a form of guidance. His mind went flat. Abe turned and started to walk away. He gave Bubby a chance to accompany him. Bubby just stood there.

Devon needed at least one of them to distract Mosely. He looked at Bubby and said, "Well?"

Abe said, "Joining this dipshit makes you one too, Bub." Bubby opened his mouth, but no words came out. He watched Abe ascend the hill and walk out of sight. Devon started spit firing plans at Bubby. It all amounted to this. Bubby was to distract Kathy for fifteen or twenty minutes while Devon stole her mom's jewelry. Not all of it of course. Then it would be obvious that it was Bubby and him. Bubby stared at Devon as the kid spoke. There was something off about the surroundings. The houses across the way seemed slumped and the buildings were about to slide down the hill and land in the creek. The tingle started again in Bubby's legs. He found himself following Redson up the hill. All his will, everything that made him *him*, was on display. Lasers would go right through him. He wasn't moving his limbs. Some outside force was doing it for him. He was not embodying himself. One little push and he'd be knocked on the ground only to find himself rolling down the hill and splashing into Stone Creek.

But there they were, ambling forward. "I just remembered…" Bubby said, but his words caught in the wind and the rain. Devon didn't even turn back. Devon goes this way, Devon turns right here, and Bubby dumbly follows. Kathy's house loomed in the near distance.

Kathy came to the door and Devon turned on the charm. Bubby was more worried about what to say to the girl than the actual danger he would be in if he stayed to do the crime. The place smelled like any house that wasn't yours. Different and unclassifiable. Bubby was trying to come up with something to say as Devon moved through the house. Kathy had a vacant look in her eyes. Bubby wanted to scream call the cops, now, Kathy, Devon's up to no good. She invited him to come into the living room. She was watching TV, she said. Kathy looked over her shoulder. "He's been in the bathroom for a while," she said.

Bubby grunted. He was being watched by people with binoculars in the neighboring houses. He was behind those glasses looking at himself sitting in the room. All he saw was a vacancy. Nobody home, nobody there. He could dissolve. Led in five directions at once. There was nothing to him or in him. At least he was aware of the problem, he told himself, a positive. Kathy made a move to get up, when Devon came into the room, his backpack on his back. Bubby wasn't in control of the part of his brain that controlled speech. He'd had his insides removed.

"We'll be going now, Kathy," Devon said.

"Oh?"

"See you first period."

Devon and Bubby were at the door. Bubby opened his mouth and muttered, "So, sorry." To Kathy's ears it sounded like a bunch of slurred S's.

Bubby woke up a little past noon. He got up and looked out his window. Pop music came from the kitchen. He began mouthing the words to the song. His music, his decade, his time. He wondered if Mrs. Mosely had discovered the missing jewelry, conferred with her daughter who fingered him and Devon for the theft. All quiet so far.

Carrie Welter was singing along to the song. Bubby knew she was off key. But, how much though? He went back and threw himself down on the bed. He picked up the book they were reading for English. The blandness of the picture on the cover was enough to make him sick with boredom. He read a sentence or two of the back cover then let the book drop to the floor. He was going to pay for his sloth. It became this whisper from within. Bubby groaned and rose from the bed.

She was looking through the packet. "Hey, Bub. There's French toast." Bubby's hunger came alive at the smell and sight of the battered bread. He turned on the skillet and greased it with butter. He placed three pieces of bread on it and listened to the sizzle. He gazed hungrily at the bread frying on the skillet. His mother started whistling. Bubby looked over at her and smiled. The song playing now no doubt brought her back. He put the pieces of bread on a plate and took them to the kitchen table. The redness was gone from her face. She had a bounce this morning.

"There're a couple of places out on Falls and a few on River and out at Seneca Hills. You'll take a ride out there, won't you, Bub?" Bubby poured a river of syrup over his French Toast, so that the bread was now drowning.

"I…uh…"

"Come on! What else do you have to do?"

He opened his mouth so he could proclaim his feigned plans. Nothing came out.

"You'll come then. It'll be your house, too." His mother was good at offering him a choice without giving him any options. He buried his head in the toast. Then he got the urge to confess.

"Me and this kid Devon. We, uh…" Lucky for him she wasn't even listening. She was deep in her dreams. He took a bite. "How did Grandpa get all the money?"

"He owned a roofing company."

Bubby looked at her, actually got a chance to study her. It

made no sense. Bubby knew how expensive the properties were out where they were going house hunting that day.

"But that surely couldn't have been…you know, enough."

"Stop asking questions, Bubby." Carrie lit a cigarette and took a prodigious drag. The sky outside was grey and mournful. She blew a tube of smoke out of her mouth. A heavy tiredness fell on the boy. He wanted to be on the couch, tube blaring, hands in his pants.

"I think I'll hold down the fort today."

"You'll do nothing of the sort. Go and put on those new pants and shirt and get yourself together. How do you want to go through life? Unprepared, or ready for battle? Lift the curtains, Bub. Get out of your funky funk. We all are rooting for you." *We all?* She became even more animated, talking of plans and courses of action. It all washed over him. She was up now, gesticulating. He could cover his ears or jump out the window. Or both. Out the window with his ears covered. What would Swanson across the hall make of all this? *Maybe he owned a gun I could borrow.*

They got in the car and drove down a length of the Canal. Animals were lined up against the side of the road peering into the car. Eventually they would surround their vehicle and make their play. The car would be nudged and prodded and it would be overturned. Antlers would scratch and thump against the windows. Bubby was trying to be as observant as humanly possible, alert to his mother's movements behind the wheel, her smoking, her incessant, controlling speech. Bubby dreamed of being older, but again, was stuck with the feeling that he'd become an overgrown lump of sod.

"We'll get a bite in town," she said. "You'll get something

healthy, Bub. We can't have you getting any bigger." His insides began to blare. He could reach over and yank the steering wheel toward him sending the car into the Canal. The get out of being her son card well played. "You've been going to the gym after school, right?" Bubby ate his tongue.

"Yeah," he said with such a lack of enthusiasm that his mother couldn't make out the words.

"We'll get a bite in town."

"The stars are aligned," his mother said. "Everything's going to fall into place. We'll get you into one of these good high schools. You'll meet new friends. We'll get you onto the right track." Bubby remembered Abe calling him a douchebag for going along with Redson. He wanted to make things right. "Now, let's do this," she was saying. "Let's go in with a strategy." They parked in front of the deli. Bubby made for the door handle, then looked over at his mother. It got started. "I can't," she muttered. "I just can't." Her crying quickly turned into sobbing. She knocked her hands against the steering wheel. Bubby thought about being in front of the TV, when suddenly a look of concern overcame his face. *What could it be? What words could I use?* She was in the throes of it now.

"Do you have a pill?" His words were still subdued, if not wholly unintelligible. "We're looking at places, Mom. We're getting a bite in this deli." He looked at the place. "Seems like a fine establishment."

"I don't know what I'm…"

Bubby had his hands crossed behind his head, the old familiar shows alighting from the box. Then he was at Stone Creek, then at Kathy Mosely's, he was apologizing to her. He thought about Devon Redson and the idea that not everyone was born good. Bubby found a box of tissues in the glove and passed it over to his mother. "Thanks, Bub." The sobbing relented. She wiped her eyes and blew her nose, then she sat up straight. She had a wistful look on her face, but she began to utter positive phrases again. One cliché after another. Bubby only knew his mother in the way a son knows his mother. The woman was just there, keeping everything in place. She put food on the table, clothes on his back, he wasn't at all charged with really caring about her or paying attention to her moods, taking care of her even less. But she was here sitting right beside him. He was forced to care, and the fact was, he really did. Plus, if she went off the deep end, it would affect him greatly.

Once at a table in the deli, Carrie started going through the packet again. Bubby was mad at her for ordering him a salad. He saw worms writhing through the lettuce and cucumber. He cautiously spiked a piece of radish and brought it up to his nose, then his mouth. There was meat frying in the place, meat that would be laid upon a sub to make a steak and cheese. The place was filled with smoke. Bubby named the song playing, hoping to get a positive reaction from his mother, but she just sucked on her cigarette and flipped through the packet. Bubby mustered up the courage to ask his mother for something sweet.

"Out of the question," she said. Bubby's face stone. "Well," she said, "One little ice cream won't hurt." She hadn't looked at him. She pulled some money from her purse and held the bills out to Bubby. Bubby had seen this movie. He reached his hand out tentatively to grab a five, when his mother yanked the bills back. "Have an apple. You'll thank me." Carrie lit another cigarette. Bubby noticed that her hand was shaking. He had those conflicting emotions again. At once, he wanted to grab that hand and quell the trembling. On the other hand, he would let her dive into the pit she was standing over. His mother began talking again. This is how good it's going to be. "We'll make the place cozy." Her speech rushing out of her. Bubby felt it washing over him. The boy struck dumb, sitting there, nary a thought entering his head. He felt like he'd never be able to talk, listen or move again. His mother's words flying above and around him. There lifting a net trying to catch them, yet not knowing how. Powerless to stop the barrage. He fell into himself. Nothing could wake him. His eyes were glassy and far away. Bubby looked around at the people at the other tables, but he saw none of them. It came time to leave a tip. Carrie laid down six dollars, but on their way out of the place, she studied the gratuity and picked up the one.

They drove down a bucolic road lined with trees and long driveways, houses with lots of acreage. Bubby pressed his head on the window glass while his mother spoke in a rush. She talked about the necessity of bargaining and not showing herself to be too eager. They were greeted at the first house by the realtor. She was dressed smart. Her handbag matched her suit. She ushered them past the row of plants guarding the walk and into the house. It was enormous. Bubby wondered, as they moved through the spacious, empty rooms, how their measly number of belongings they owned could possibly fill this house. They'd have to start an orphanage. Carrie grew quiet as they ascended the stairway to the second floor. The master bedroom was wide and deep. Bubby studied his mother as she and the realtor discussed the complexion of the neighborhood, schools, conveniences, etc. "And it will just be you and your son living here?" There were four other bedrooms. Carrie had a grave, if not anguished look on her face. He feared an eruption. He worried about her then. Someone had to wrap their arms around her lest she crack apart.

He was glad that he could be so carried away with good feelings toward his mother. But he couldn't do anything about it just then.

Carrie was quiet still. Her face was hard. Bubby made a comment about the size of the room that the two of them decided would be his. Carrie craned her neck. Bubby expected her to blurt something out, but she remained speechless. He would miss the apartment. It had everything he needed. He wanted to take his mother by the arm and lead her back to Que Street. They were in the kitchen now. It was modern, slate island in the middle, all the flashy appliances. Bubby eyed his mother again. It was getting worse. She appeared glum and lost. In the foyer, the realtor started talking financing and prices, when Carrie opened her mouth. A hole was about to open in the floor. She'd slide down. Bubby thought that if she said a word it would put ideas in the realtor's head. Carrie was able to say, "We'll get in touch," but it sounded feeble.

There were two other houses on her list. They got in the car. Bubby was bathed in silence. He couldn't even look over at her. She turned right on Whitman. "Are we heading home, Mom?"

"Don't ask me any questions!" A shiver went through the boy. He bent down into himself and pinned his eyes on all the scenery floating by. None of it registered.

That night Bubby lay on the couch thumbing through the packet. He thought about how many boxes they would need to haul their stuff out to the burbs. He settled on twenty-three. On the screen in front of him a helicopter flew across a sea. A man was waiting on the tarmac to receive the people who climbed out of the bird. We'll get you up to speed, the man said. You'll meet Alex and Steve, the agents. Right this way. Bubby got back to the packet.

He circled the phone. It had been too long. Abe's mother answered on the third ring. He was quiet. Not a good sign. "Abraham? Look, I just want to say… I'm not in with Redson, and I'm sorry you got tangled up in all that bs." The line went cold. Bubby heard things being moved in his house.

"Cut ties with him."

"I did. I will. I feel so bad about Kathy. What we put her through."

"Well, I just wanted to see what that shit for brains had up his sleeve. Now that I know, I hate him even more."

"And me, Abe?"

Quiet again. Bubby started wrapping the phone cord around his fingers. "We're good. As long as you denounce the kid."

"Consider him denounced."

"All right, then, Bub."

"All right."

Bubby switched off the TV. Gunshots would ring, and Bub would be sprayed by swirling, errant, long-range fire. The ambulance driver wouldn't be kind on the way to the hospital. He'd have an admonishing look on his face. You play with fire, his look would say. The apartment building would burn down. Swanson would lend Bubby a sweater and all the tenants would gather outside in the cold watching their entire world burn up in flames. He'd get knifed leaving his place that Monday for school. The blade would go searching around his insides, and he'd never get a look at the guy who plunged it in. Kathy Mosely's father would show up at his door with a you're scum look on his face and a high-powered weapon resting on his shoulder. He'd mention his daughter then send a shell rocketing into Bubby's insides. It would leave a gaping hole in his midsection and his guts would pour out of his body. He'd have time even to explore his entrails as they sluiced down to the floor. Carrie would be so washed out in the other room making it impossible for her to hear the blast. Abe too. He would show up with a bow and arrow. He'd have it all cued up and standing at the door, he'd make his stand. You were never a real friend and then let fly, arrow meeting Bubby's heart. Out on the street walking, Bubby would meet passers-by, strangers, all the people, would greet him with the rudest, meanest, and most threatening glances.

    He was about to flick the TV back on again, when he heard the sobbing coming from his mother's room down the hall. He listened intently. Heaving. She was searching for air. Bubby crept down the hall. The sobbing got louder. He made himself as small and quiet as possible. All the thoughts of her being pitiable washed away. He felt this tender urge. He would wait until the sobs subsided. She was gone. Just drifted away. First, he pictured himself in an orphanage, then in foster care. That couldn't be good. He'd be raped by the father, abused by the siblings, denied his right to watch TV. Tossed and flipped up and down. He could be taken in by Swanson. He was a helpless boy standing outside the room that housed his weeping and pained mother. The uncertainty drove him nuts. The TV was still there. His mother still wept. He took a step toward her room. The sobbing hit a crescendo and then began to tail off. Bubby tried to deal with his fear. It shot through him. Made his skin prickly. He heard her get up. Bubby scurried into his room and made like he was asleep. He heard through the walls. She was rummaging through the cabinets. The itch spread through Bubby's body. He didn't have enough nails to scratch it away.

    She turned on the faucet. The water came down. He looked up at the ceiling. That's when the door opened. He closed his eyes and feigned sleep. "Bubby?" She was whispering. She said his name again. Bubby didn't move, nor did he utter a sound. "Bubby? Are you asleep." The itch. He remained quiet. Then she was gone.

Chapter 2

She lay with her knees bent, head resting on the headboard of Swanson's bed. She was a woman yearning to become pregnant, urging his sperm to make that singular journey, rooting that one champion on, then, bang, Bubby's got a sister. It was only a 1 in 14-odd million chance. How did this happen? One minute they were exchanging pleasantries in the foyer of the building and the next he was groping and nuzzling her breasts up in his place, 3A. She could kill for a cigarette. When he came back from the bathroom, she had time to inspect his knees. They poked her when they were engaged in the love act. And the size of him. It made her hurt in places with names that couldn't come to her. He bent over the bed and pulled the covers over Carrie's upper body. He stared at her for a moment. She smiled weakly and said, "What?"

"I've got to get to work now."

Carrie thought about the trip out to the suburbs two days before. She mused on the state of her mind. There were a thousand things she should be taking care of but was at pains to start the list.

"What's your first name?"

Swanson looked puzzled, as if he'd forgotten. He had piercing, slate grey eyes. And now that she had been intimate with him, she could see him more clearly. He looked younger than what his age probably was. She leaned toward him. He studied her face, then looked toward the den, remembering something. He still had a full head of hair, salt and pepper, the grey stippled on the sides of his head. She saw his alertness, the effortless gestures, and the wiriness. He had to be fifty-five, sixty, tops, but he looked like he was in his forties. He could have been climbing out of foxholes in Korea, or holding signs up in the late '60s. A feeling of contentment washed over her. This might have been the invitation to start up again.

"Anthony," he said. "Tony Swanson." He looked into her eyes. This sent shockwaves through her.

"Carrie," she said. "Carrie Welter."

"We both know these things. We're living on top of each other, and yet never took the chance to get to know one another."

He leaned in and pecked her on the cheek out of some fake masculine duty. He was in boxer shorts and a T-shirt. She raised herself up and pulled off her top. Her kiss was more alive now. Before it started, he looked up and to his left. Something lined up in his head, but it got thrown off course at the sight of Carrie Welter.

They lay in the afterglow. "You don't smoke, do you?" During, she'd lost herself. Her tangled mind was smoothed out. How long would that feeling last? The sense of chaotic urgency was returning.

"No. But, go ahead."

He got up and rummaged through the drawers in the kitchen. His backside was held together, she noticed. Nothing in the way of sag. He returned with an ashtray, and she put flame to cigarette end. The cherry igniting on the long, hard pull. It was new. The first one she'd ever had. Standing behind Betty Jumper's house, just in front of the tool shed. It hurt. And so did the second one. But like all consummate smokers she was persistent.

"I'm working on a project," he said. "Pictures and words."

He was up putting on his pants.

"You'll get it published?"

"I haven't thought that far in advance yet." He scratched at the hair hanging over a temple. "I'm trying to remember. But, when I do, I just start making it all up."

"You have intelligent eyes," she said. Tony looked away from her. He lifted his head up again. Up and to the left. Remembering something.

"I won't keep you. I have a million things to do." She started on a mental list and got stuck at one: get back to my place across the hall. "There's no end to it." The desperation and futility squeezed by her lips. Tony Swanson looked at her, then turned away. His moustache jumped a little, and the prickly hairs brushed his nostrils.

"Thank you for the compliment, Carrie." She leaned forward. *Give me something*, she thought. *Take me somewhere. Light me up in fire and then douse me with a firehose.*

"We're moving to the suburbs." It came out in a rush, and in the form of a half question. She was seeking permission. Carrie took a long drag and let the smoke caress, corrode her lungs. It had been a while, and she wondered how it was going to go. He'd swiftly gotten her from the mailroom up into his apartment.

"Oh?"

"It's pretty out there and the schools are good, and Bubby will make friends quick." Again, she was trying to have her doubts mollified. She thought of the few houses they had looked at and cringed when she imagined the way her mind and body went into lockdown out there. How Bubby had to talk her down.

"It'll be good for the boy. The city's crumbling."

Carrie didn't answer and his comment hung in the air.

She looked up at him in a dreamy way. Part admiration, part

little girl looking for something from her long-gone father. He searched his lap. "I've thought about you."

Carrie looked out the window. A tree branch was trying to scratch the glass. How did the tree get up this high? "Now."

"It's true."

Carrie gnawed at the insides of her cheeks. She could make a fool of herself. This would ice it. Flounce into the bathroom and weep like a junior high school girl. You don't love me. It's impossible. You can't love me. The branches scraped.

"Look, Carrie."

"Hmm-hmm?" There was an edge to her voice. He put up a hand and pressed it down to ease things off.

Here she went.

Tony got up and put on a button-down shirt. He flicked his stubble with the back of his fingers. Turned back to look at her. She had lain back down on the bed. Something in her eyes. The pupils had taken over the whole of them. Alert. Frenzied.

"Carrie, listen. I don't mean to throw you out, but I've really got to get to work."

She pouted, then quickly tried to cover it up. The walk across the hall would be a slog.

"All right, all right."

He stopped and took her in. Tony Swanson used all his height and stillness to coax her toward the door. Carrie was trying her hardest not to display the catastrophe she thought she was. "We can have dinner," he said. "Then we can talk."

"Can you turn around?" She got up and put her clothes on. At the door, she pivoted and scanned the living room. "I'll see you, Ton. I know where to find you." Tony did his best to smile. And then she was gone.

She made the walk of ten feet across to her apartment, still glowing, yet something more odious creeping through her. It had been a while. Tony had eased something off in her. Back in her apartment, the glow was extinguished. She collapsed onto the sofa and began biting her nails. She felt strangely angry, as if she might hurt herself or bust up something in her apartment. Folded her hands. Cracked her knuckles. In the bathroom investigating the wrinkles that were beginning to form around her eyes. Thirty-three going on fifty-three. The cycle would spin her right into fragility and old age, and it would happen rapidly. She saw herself going out the door and making the ten-foot run to Tony's. Beating back the thoughts. Worthless. Lost. Inept. She went into the living room and put on a record. The guitar cried and it made her weep just the same. Open the window. Shimmy out. She'll go to the drawer in the kitchen. Then, she thought about Bub. She made a pact with herself. Bub, and only Bub.

Tony went into his den and started sorting the Polaroids he'd taken. He picked up the first one. It was of an Oak tree down at Stone Creek. He picked up the glue and dabbed some on the back, then stuck it in the next empty page of the album. A flash of Carrie Welter, skin on skin. She took him down, away. Now it was the photo. He studied it for a few minutes, waiting for his thoughts to align with his eyes. The tree he'd climbed in the backyard. His father's arms reaching up to catch him when he jumped. A fearlessness. The future and the past meant nothing to him. The world of doubts and adult responsibilities even less. The adrenaline took care of that. Was there a girl with him? When he got older? Yes, there was a girl. Her name was…what was her name? He couldn't for the life of him remember. Sitting in the tree with the no named girl, he wrote. No fear, no past, no future, unable to conjure up regrets. I didn't even know what the word meant. He wrote. I can just see what's right in front of me. And I get up on the thick branch and I jump.

Picking through the small stack of photos. One caught his eye. It was a park bench empty of things and people. He picked it up and studied it. Tony took a deep breath and tried to clear his mind of all thoughts. He closed his eyes. The blackness enveloped him. It worked for nearly a minute. And then these thoughts. Try to remember, then learn to forget. Into them, up, out, back, relinquish. The blackness returned. He folded his arms on the desk. The park bench was a refuge, a place of rest. He wrote that sentence down under the photo after he had glued it to the page. In the bathroom peeing, thoughts rushed. He was running around a track. The headlines in the newspaper were dire. There was talk of this nation entering the war. On the track, he thought of his mother, her nose plastered to the radio, a crispness in his father's voice. "He's too young, Donna." And Tony ran, arms pumping, legs lifting. He was safe. The clouds and their soft outlines and puffy insides sheltered him. He ran like the wind pushing those clouds.

The mind is not a racetrack, Tony thought, as he washed his hands in the sink. *It is a cloud. Mutable.* He didn't write these lines under the photo of the park bench. He jotted them down in a notebook he had beside the album. Again, the darkness overtook his mind. When he came to, he was lifting the album up so he could study the photo of the park bench. He was going down to the bus depot to deliver his father's lunch pail to him. In a rush to get out of the house his father had forgotten it. Tony was no more than ten, and the task filled him with magnanimity. His father had patted him on the back. He said some kind words to the boy. Then he was on the bus bench waiting for the 35 north.

This is what he wrote under the photo of the park bench. It was a refuge, a place of rest, the hope of a destination: Duty done. I'm going home.

Tony got up and turned on the radio to the jazz station. He went to the window and looked down on Que. The tree branches obscured his vision slightly. He watched the people go by, all bundled in winter coats. A deep sadness descended on him. The saxophone blew a mournful wail. The sudden thought that nothing matters. The will folding in on itself. A ball in his hollow chest bouncing around. The feeling, always ephemeral, took him down anyway. He went into his bedroom and dug the photos out of the drawer. There she was in all her beauty. He hadn't seen his daughter in five years. Last they'd talked she was living in the Midwest with a man she'd met. It was possible that that had gone south, and that she had dropped him and left. She had a wild streak that he was mostly at pains to tame. Tony stared at the photo of her. He rubbed his fingers over Ashley's face and body. A wistful net dropped over him. He felt his insides go soft.

The day was a tunnel he had to crawl through. Was there a ray of light at the end that could be its reward? He took off his clothes and inspected his face in the mirror. Then he got in the shower and let the hot water beat down on him. Her skin, her touch. The foreignness of it all. How it thrust him back. It was urgent and unexpected and thrilling. Try to remember, learn to forget. Bring it up anew. He got dressed and grabbed the camera from the table. He gazed at her door – thoughts of how to peel away his loneliness and face the world – then opened it, damn it all, and went down the stairs.

He was eating a sandwich at the counter of the place down on Row Street called Scott's. The camera rested in his little black bag. What he thought and felt about his daughter. That there was always time to repair. To set things right. He couldn't think of what there was to set right, though. Time and missed opportunities – personality clash? – had separated them. There wasn't a big blow-up or a transgression or even a small fight. She grew up and went out into the world and their relationship just eked away. Nobody was at fault. But, there had to be something he had done wrong. He held his sandwich in the air about to gesticulate with it, make a speech to the other diners. Something was going to make him leap up and run back to his place to start writing the letter. He took a bite of his food. Then another one. The nutrients calmed him. He paid his check and went out into the day. The sky helped him along, a blue, tinted with winterly white, that enveloped, a sign that he should move.

He walked across the barren softball diamond. A sliver of the Camotop in the distance. The water pushing its way toward the Bay. He got to the playground and took out his camera. He always made sure that there weren't people in the photos he took. And now there were two little tots scampering and bouncing around the apparatuses. Afraid that he'd be seen as a stalker, or worse, he ambled toward the church on the other side of the playground. He took a picture of the steeple.

God wanted something from him. Cannot put you in words. He asked from him mercy and forgiveness and compassion. Tough order. Could he hold up his end of the bargain? Tony remembered holding his father's hand in church, settling on the word 'meek'. Then his mind and entire body going into a fidget. The short walk home. The best part, father taking his time, talking about everything and nothing at all. The hands clasped. In the pool of joy. Mother with all the things she had to do on her mind, hurrying ahead. His father behind the newspaper. It was all about getting his attention. I'll do it, Dad, I'll turn the other cheek, even if I don't know what it means. Just put the newspaper down. Tony looked up and saw a flock of birds trying to warm themselves up on this winter day, not sure if they had lost the rest of their flock and had missed the chance to fly south, stuck forever in this cold place. Their flapping surely generated heat.

He found himself making his way down the hill toward the river, his bag tucked snugly around his shoulder, clinging to his side. Her skin. The look in her eyes. The friction less in his mind than the feel of her warmth. It had been so long. Did he make a mockery of himself? Fail to please her correctly? Acted like an old codger? And then her head turned away. She was in a distant place, and he had to pull her back to where they were. He shook his head. He told himself not to forget this, knowing full well that it would fade. He had enough memories that he was trying to make vanish. Why not hold onto her skin? The soft porcelain.

Tony walked the footpath by the river. He was out in the field serving a directive. The sun was trying to reveal itself. He unwrapped his scarf and then rewrapped it around his neck. Taking pictures was stealing. It was an imposition, it blinded one's sight. Writing was theft, too. Appropriating from other sources. Finding the means to be original. It arrived and then departed. The world got in your head, and you spit its fragments out on the page, in conversation. The river was making its way south. Tony found a picnic table. The bridge to remember—that was the name—off in the distance, telling us to never forget. But we do. We are in a collective mind warp making it impossible to learn anything about the past, and we make the same mistakes repeatedly.

A few stubborn fishermen in jackets and hats with their lines hanging optimistically in the water. An airplane overhead, banking, following the curve of the river. Ashley was a quiet girl. It took her longer than the other kids to get going. She had this reticence. On many occasions, she declined invitations to birthday parties and the like, no matter how eagerly and patiently her mother coaxed her into going. It'll be fun. She made friends in high school and began to come out of her shell. Then she exploded. It was as if this molten lava ran under the outwardly shy girl. Tony and his wife lost track of her for a while after she'd dropped out of college. He supposed she fell into the morass of the deadening counterculture of the '70s. She unraveled, no doubt, with the rest of society. The pain of all the hope and goodwill shot down like those leaders. He got a letter from her in the early '80s. It was erratic. She was angry and was trying to prove some kind of point. He saw her in '83. She came east. She was looking for work. Ashley had that burned out look from drugs. But there was something more to it. They talked for an hour, she fidgeted and paced a lot, and then she was off. I'm going to get my degree, and he waited for it. And then it came. Just a little to get me over the hump. His love for her and this strange sense of guilt – even if he had no reason to feel guilty – overcame him. He found himself writing a check for $1,000. Was it enough to appease the sensation? She kissed him on the cheek and then strolled out into the humid afternoon. Tony sat there and felt his insides being torn to shreds. In his mind, he was tearing out of the place, running after her. To say what? How on earth did he let this happen? She was a baby once; one he'd held in his arms. And now this.

Tony went soft. Right there on the bench. All mush. He knew what he had to do. One of the fishermen was hauling in a Rockfish and Tony felt like clapping. He had the address, knowing full well that it could have stopped being hers years ago.

He got up and started walking the footpath. To his left, the parks led to the granite of the monuments and statues. Did two horse legs in the air signify that the soldier had died in battle? He couldn't remember and it bothered him for a minute. The bridge rose to his left. Cars rolled east and west. He waited for the traffic to cease. The J. Center shone to his left. There was a gap in the traffic. Tony snapped off three pictures and shook them in the breeze. They told him something, but he'd have to get back to the quiet of his apartment to analyze them further. The bridge seemed to be swaying as he stood on it staring into the muck of the river. He took a picture of the little island in the water. Then a shot of a plane soaring overhead. Flapping the "negatives" in the wind. A boat made its way toward the bridge. Too many people on board, the vessel sagging. He was writing the letter in his mind, knowing full well its addressee would never see it. There was never any drama until she became an adult. Then she left and all her endeavors became a secret. Still, he gave her money. Father making moves to invite her back into his life. At Margaret's funeral, but that's seven years ago. She looked washed out, either from grief or illicit substances, or both. Tony made his way toward the footpath again. He suddenly thought of another way. There were a couple of women friends of Ashley's who might know where she was. If the letter bounced back, he'd get in touch with them.

    He was at the war memorial. The dark granite funneling people through the horrors, prompting them to think, to remember. All the names engraved in the black. He stopped, put his camera down and went up and ran his hands over some of the names. The presence of other people, mostly tourists, kept his emotions from getting away from him. He put his hand under his chin and let it come anyway. A shudder and then a tear forming in his eye. *We learn nothing. It's an endless cycle.* He was self-conscious about the cheapness of his Polaroid. He made his way back toward home. He took a picture of a statue, his hands sure on the camera, on the red button.

The building there on the hill. Once inside, he took a bottle of beer out of the fridge and sat down at his desk in the den. All the photos and the words were there, faithfully, and dutifully awaiting his return. He put the new ones down on the pile. He took a sip of beer and then invited the blackness in again. He closed his eyes and maneuvered within the dark of his mind. A spot of light, then nothing again. Thoughts arriving then beaten back. The demands of the world. He opened his eyes and looked out the window. The suds of the beer went down well. He took another sip, then picked up the photo of the bridge. He wrote these words on his pad. *How do we get there from here, and what is holding us up?* He looked at the photo of the river he took from the bridge. *The water is spirit, the current too, carrying and moving constantly, and yet, I will never know how or why.* Tony closed his eyes again and felt the presence of Ashley in the blackness. Memories came to him. The shy girl whom he'd tried to extract from her room. The reckless teenager not taking any crap from anyone. The transformations. The moods. The growth – from what to what? The missteps. Wrong words spoken.

Once again, slipping into the dark. Vague notions. Creeping thoughts, then black again. He was sweeping the thoughts through his mind, not getting attached to any of them. The sky was darkening out the window.

He found the last address he had for her in his book. Then he got up and put on a blues record, stood in the middle of his living room feeling the pain of every lost soul. That was washed away and so went his inspiration and sense of brotherly love. It wasn't ill-will that he felt, it was loss and emptiness. He sat down on the sofa and drank his beer. 44 G Street. He ran his hand over the name of the city and the zip.

He wrote the letter. He focused on maintaining a cordial, caring tone. It's been too long, Ashley. I would like to know what is happening in your life. You mean so much to me. I desperately want to reconnect. Is it possible for us to meet? I would love to see you, to hear about you. I miss you terribly. Enough? He folded the letter and placed it in the envelope, wrote her address and his in the corner, careful to write as legibly as possible. He drained the beer, then stood and changed the record. She was all alone out there. He could shrivel up.

The pile of photos were an affront. Set them on fire. Crying for her and for so much more. There was no stopping it now. He didn't care to pull himself together. He let it all flow. And then the black. There on the sofa he let the dark surround him. No need to analyze or figure anything out. Just a pool of darkness.

Bubby was in the kitchen doing his math homework or at least pretending to do his math homework. He was tapping his pencil against the book. His mother sat across from him, annoyed by the tapping. She had a brochure for the adult learning annex in front of her, idly thumbing through pages with the different courses listed on them. "Accounting! I was always good with numbers." Bubby stole a glance at her. "History! No, that won't get me anywhere. I need something practical. Secretarial!" Bubby stole a glance at her. He watched his mother's face droop. She put the brochure down and lit a cigarette from the lit end of the last one. Swanson's moustache brushing up against her face. She glanced at the door, measured the number of steps it would take her to cross the hall, pictured his face in her mind. She couldn't do it.

She couldn't arrange his features correctly. But she could feel him. The pleasure and the agony and the feel of his body encroaching upon her own. The paper lay on the coffee table. Want ads picking on her. A deep drag from her butt. "Yes! Bub, the world is my oyster." He studied her. She looked at more of the ads as Bub watched her face turn morose. "Oh, no! I don't have any experience in that field. I'd have to go back to school."

The more Bubby thought he was vacant and unable to come up with original thoughts, the more his mind was producing them.

He was still working on the same problem. Just when he thought he had it, it slipped through his mind. He looked over at her. She was bent over seemingly picking up a dust bunny. He'd call Abe and see what he was up to. They could sit on his stoop and watch the people go by. He looked at his mother. She was a shell of a woman. Bubby felt angry. He wanted to punch something. "Do you want pork chops or soup, Bub?" Bubby looked at her stone faced. Before he had a chance to answer, his mother proclaimed, "Pork chops it is then."

Bubby said, "Whatever," under his breath.

Carrie Welter was off on some distant planet where all the norms were alien to her. She got up and turned on the oven while Bubby sank desperately into his math homework. He was in remedial math, but they had mercy on those in the class not to call it that. He was getting nowhere. He was working on word problems: a train going 90 mph arrives at the station at five p.m., etc. He wanted to be on that train. All his troubles going by the window, left behind. He looked at his mother's back as she stood laboring over the stove. That anger arose again. He didn't realize that whom he was angry with was himself. *Boxcars: I am a hobo.* A glorious world of freedom. Release from his shoehorned existence.

He called Abe after dinner. Bubby put on his jacket and made for the front door. Carrie was there in a flash. He picked up that mad glow in her eyes. "Back by eleven." She was right up close to him. He could make out the eyeliner around her eyes, see that it was painted on. Scents he couldn't name. "Well, I guess it's just me on my own." Her eyes drilled into Bubby's. He felt immobilized. She was quiet, and when she was, it held all kinds of portents.

"I could..." Bubby started to say something but couldn't finish his thought. Her look made him freeze up. How to wiggle out of her guilt trip.

Carrie paced for a minute. She bit a nail and spit it out. She wanted him on the couch. The comfort of another human body in the house, living and breathing. Not able to withstand the quiet, the ticking of the clock, all the desperation. "No, tell Abe's mother I said hi." Carrie had the reproachful look on the woman's face in her mind when Bubby mentioned her name. "I'm going to keep going on these help wanted ads." This only made Bubby feel guiltier. He dropped his hand from the doorknob. Anything could happen. The woman could shatter and be whipped around in a breeze, all the pieces of her swirling around, he'd try to reach up and gather them, to reassemble them, her. "Go! What are you waiting for?" Bubby knew how hard it was to be a single parent. He wanted to tell her this, but he didn't have the words for it just then. *I'm on your side, Mom. Know that.* Bubby sheepishly turned away from his mother and went for the doorknob again. He was halfway out when Carrie came over and stood in the gap the door made. She followed him mentally down the first set of stairs. He could feel her eyes pinned on him. Bubby stopped and dared himself to look back up. Was she shaking? The indecision he felt was like a flu. Then she brushed at him with a hand and closed the door on him. Was it a slam? On the inside of the apartment, Carrie leaned against the door and did all she could not to slide down it. After a moment of wallowing, she went into the bathroom and fixed her hair, did a touch up with some make up, peed, washed her hands, then marched to the door. She flung her door open and took two strident, marching steps toward Tony's, then crumbled and returned to the safety of her own apartment.

Abe had a concerned look on his face. "I want to out this Redson kid." They were sitting on the stoop of his family's townhouse. It was something they did, night or day. At the sound of Redson's name, Bubby went numb. *Then, I am outed*, he thought.

"He's all right," Bubby said, trying to save his own ass. "Despite…" He didn't have the syntactical skills to complete the thought.

Abe glowered at him. "You said you were done with him."

"I am done with him."

"You've got this thing you do, Bub."

Bubby looked at Abe. "Yeah, you mumble something under your breath. Then you squeeze out a little laugh. It makes you look like you lack conviction."

The anger in Bubby got covered by this film. He couldn't imagine his brain making thoughts. "I, uh. Yeah, he's a lout, and I'm done with him."

"Well, you're lucky you and him didn't go down on the Kathy Mosely thing."

"Hey, there's your neighbor."

Bubby watched Swanson take a left on 27th. He was holding

a letter in his hand. Tony found the box on the corner and dropped it in. He then started walking toward the stoop Abe and Bubby were sitting on. "Hi, Mr. Swanson."

"Bubby. How are you?"

"This is Abe."

"Hello, Abe. What's up fellas?" Bubby immediately recognized that this was what a geyser like Swanson would say to a couple of teenagers. Right from his shows. Jump in fellas, there's room in the back.

"Just taking in the view," Abe said.

"Yeah, taking in the view," Bubby said, then instantly castigated himself.

"Well, I'm off," Swanson said. He continued down Pine Street.

Carrie was working on her courage. She'd been to the door three times now. Got it opened and managed two steps across the hall before turning around. She smoked a cigarette, hoping it would give her the final inch of wherewithal. Three steps across the landing this time, then stiffened. Three more. Her finger wandering over the bell, hitting it. No answer. She rang again. Her hands were balled. She thought about his hands, those parts of him slapping against her upper thighs, him pressing into her, grabbing her sides, kissing her, his touch, the reprieve from her silenced life. One more ring. Then she was banging on his door. Really letting it have it. Rap, rap, rap. Bang, bang, bang. She couldn't catch herself. *I'm making a mess again.* Returning to her apartment and stopping herself from slamming the door. At first, she was angry, then she just became goop. In the kitchen sobbing and berating herself. The emotions were alive, lit and tumbling through her. What's the use? She said aloud. The kitchen table a refuge, nicotine and tar, chain-smoking the rest of her pack.

Tony walked down Pine and made a left on R. He wondered how Ashley would react to his letter if it even reached her. She was out on a winter's night, no shelter in sight, just a lost young woman beaten down, surrounded by bad actors. Tony told himself to snap out of it. She had resourceful qualities. It wasn't the catastrophe he was making it out to be. Bring it back. And then thoughts of his role in the drama of his daughter's life. He got to U and made a right. His leather jacket felt too tight. He noticed how garbage bags were piling up on the curbs, their detritus often spilling out onto the sidewalk. He passed four men huddled together no doubt getting a false sense of warmth from the weed they were smoking and the liquor they were putting down. Tony ducked into a Middle Eastern shop and stood in line. The place was loud. When he got to the counter he had to shout to be heard. He ordered a falafel and waited outside for it to be prepared. The neighborhood throbbed. Only seventeen years before, this entire place was in flames. Scared human beings giving into their anger. He saw it all in his mind's eye. One man shot, a spark, a conflagration. Many other causes as to why this went on. Tony got all of them but didn't understand completely, he couldn't. He thought about the predicament of the other, the stepped on, the left out. Those nights he skirted the riots. Hanging back, not taking any pictures. Aghast and terrified. Back on the roof he started taking pictures of the flames, people throwing Molotov cocktails out of windows. And what did the riots result in? Look at this place.

He went in and got his food. The white sauce dribbled down his fingers as he ingested the falafel, vegetables, and pita bread.

He ate his food slowly. Then he dropped the paper in a

garbage can. Police sirens wailed as he made his way east. He checked his jacket pocket for the ticket. People were getting ready for the night. A fuse about to be lit. He should have been wary. But he moved with a surety. Longing for the heat and the music. He got to the 11:30 Club. The line was filled with the types of people that matched the kind of music that would be played that night. Tony put his hands in his pockets. A girl with a bevy of rings and spikes in her face was using the wall of the building to hold herself up. Tony saw Ashley again. Out there, alone, and scared. Other than that, most of the people in line were calm and seemingly sober. He got to the door. A burly guy with a tattoo on his neck, which he was surely careful to display, took his ticket. Tony was enveloped by the thrumming as he moved to coat check.

Abe and Bubby were still on the stoop. It had gotten colder, and they could see their breath. "My ass is getting numb," Abe said. "Let's go down to Scott's and get something good." Bubby went blank. "Bub? You with me here?"

"Yeah, yeah, I'm with you." Abe shook his head.

"Wake up, then. I asked you something."

"Yeah, Scott's."

"Come on, man. Look alert."

The anger did its work inside Bubby. "Enough." It came out so soft and weak that Bubby wasn't really sure he'd said it at all.

Abe got up and headed for the door. "I'm going in to get a five."

Bubby sulked on his own on the stoop. The thoughts came through the fog. He wanted to make everything right in one fell swoop. Save his mom, save himself, enter a new existence, change everything, become a new person altogether. He pounded his fist in his other hand and spit on the pavement.

Carrie paced every inch of the apartment. Swanson was in there. He was ignoring her. Over there again; inhibitions slinking away. A small part of her said it was going way over the line, but she ignored that impulse. There she was banging and slamming. Nilsen's door opening from downstairs. She banged one more time for good measure then slinked back into her apartment. Loneliness could not be endured. It beat down on her skull. She lit a cigarette, took a drag, then put it out, only to light another one right away. She threw the dining room window open and stuck her head out. Then she got out on the fire escape and looked down. In her mind she was already over. Nothing could stop the fall. She was about to get up on the railing. The fall would be spectacular, and then the crunch. All her bones reduced to dust. A driving pain was shooting through her. The night was alive, the darkness of the trees, the other buildings, the possibility that there were no more possibilities. This is where it comes to a screeching halt. She was already falling, floating out of this existence. Her fear, and the face of her son pulled her back.

In the kitchen rummaging pill bottles. Too many into the palm of her hand; gulping them all down. Carrie sat in front of the TV. The sounds and images did nothing for her. She patted her knees and rose. One more time. Halfway across the hall, not afraid of Nilsen from down below. She lifted her fist to rap on Tony's door but couldn't complete the action. Back in her apartment, on the couch, the sobs came. She convulsed. A fierce cry, a plea to be released. The tightness in her chest. The thoughts going round and round. She couldn't put a stop to it. Back on the fire escape. It was the image of her son that stopped her once again. Bub. The sobs came again. She went into her bedroom and lay down. The ceiling, the sky, were about to fall. Back to the pill bottles. Fifteen minutes later, she was comatose on the couch.

Chapter 3

Bubby trudged up the steps of Carter and felt his insides go soft. Truant officers all over him. He was going to be outfitted in an orange jumpsuit. That's what it was. A prison. Could being locked up be a better option? Mosely facing him in court, the verdict coming down. Abe came down the hall. Then Redson. Redson winked at Bubby and Bubby's mind turned to sludge. Abe glared at Redson. He didn't give a damn, and he wouldn't be pulled in. Bubby envied his friend. He wondered where his courage came from. His ability to flip the bird at this putz. Redson looked back and smiled. Abe slapped Bubby on the shoulder. "Get your head out of your ass, Bub."

"Yeah."

"Why do I even bother?" Abe said, then he trailed off.

Bubby was staring out the window in the back of his English class. He didn't realize that Mr. Bromberg was asking him a question until almost too late. "Say something about the irony in the opening lines." Bubby was shot through with static.

"I, uh..." The word irony shot him blind, deaf, and mute.

Bromberg shook his head and redirected the question to Amy Berman, an astute girl who sat in the front row. She came up with something pertinent, while Bubby felt the shame and embarrassment tear at him.

In the hall. Redson was on him. He told Bubby about the hold up. How it would go down. The take, the thrill, the whole thing, all its particulars. He had the store on 6th all scoped out and "Bubby, let's meet after school and cook it all up." Bubby looked at Redson, but he didn't see him. He knew he was supposed to say something, but for the life of him he couldn't come up with anything. "You're integal to all this." Integal, irony. What was going on?

"Yeah, Devon." Lead me into it he must have thought.

"Good. My father's got the iron and I'm going to jack it."

Integal, irony, iron, jack it. Bubby had come across none of these words on the cop shows he watched.

Bubby slipped away. He fell into a blank stare. "Stay with me, here Welter. After school. Down at Stone."

If Bubby had the wherewithal, he'd really start hating himself, questioning it all. He took a few steps away from Redson, then turned and looked back. Redson was making a gun out of his fingers.

Bubby just walked out the door. Fifteen minutes later, he was on his couch, TV telling him what to think or how not to think. It was that show about the taxi drivers, all of them huddled in the dispatch talking about all their intrigues. The hodgepodge of eccentric characters and the jokes all lost on the boy. There were kids left behind in that prison called school and Bub had a laugh over them. Cutting school wouldn't cause too much guilt.

Carrie was at the adult learning annex. She was wandering the halls, looking at bulletins. A layer of discomfort would come and go in her. At one point she had the urge to vomit. She settled on the notice for a history class. *You like history*. Exploring other worlds. She wrote down the information in her notebook. She looked down the halls and saw other adults moving ant-like. Her heart began to twist in her chest. And then a notice for an economics class. She went to the bursar's office and jotted her name down. Her face went hard. She couldn't see and she couldn't feel. Her words came out in soup. She was aware of the feeling but not the root causes of the fear. But sign up for the class she did.

The sun was going down when she left the building. Bubby was watching TV. Carrie urged him to get cracking on his homework. She went to the cabinets and popped a few pills. The boy watched her back. She caught fire, the flames melting her down into her shoes. He was on a bus this time traveling west, his bag on the seat next to him. The warm breeze coming through the windows as they neared the coast. Then standing on the beach watching the waves come in. Wading in in his clothes. Washing all that made up his life far, far away, out of him. New, he would think, I am new.

She entered the room, squashing his reverie. Carrie Welter was an imposition. Bubby lay and thought about the holdup he'd be doing with Devon Redson, pictured the look on Abe's face. The orange jumpsuit draped over his body, this time for real. The math homework splayed out in front of him and the migraine it was going to induce. Monkeys were banging drums in his neck. The problems were all unsolvable. He slapped his pencil against his neck to alleviate the pain. He thought he had solved the first two problems. The first ones were always the easiest ones. Everybody knew that.

Was there something to at least being aware of this type of hare-brained thinking?

The math problems got harder, and Bubby gave up. His mother had retreated to her room. The boy found shelter in his room. Locked the door. He wasn't supposed to do that, Mother's orders. First it was Berta Stowe's face and thighs that poured into his head. His hand explored, then got to work. Tracey, Melinda, his Western Civ teacher, a panoply of other females, Regina, Davida, Morgana… he recited their names, as their bodies came into view. He was done in less than a minute.

Carrie came out and knocked on her son's door. No response. She banged harder. "I'm sleeping, Mom."

The knocking slowed. Carrie went into the bathroom and did herself up as best as she could. Five minutes later, she was standing at the front door with a mangled look on her face. She imagined the prior lovemaking. I'm buying a house in the suburbs. The lie of it. She saw the distant look on his face, after, when it was done. Carrie put her hand on the doorknob and gave it a squeeze. She was now standing in the hall, one foot leading to Tony's, one back to the safety, safety? Of her apartment.

No turning back now. She was ringing the bell. There he was. Tall and a little unkempt, trying to smile.

"Carrie."

"Tony." It came out in a rush.

A moment of silence. She peered into his apartment wondering if he was housing a tiger in a cage.

"Come on in."

She gingerly entered the apartment. For a man on his own, the place radiated a calm cleanliness.

"How's the experiment?"

"Writing and photo project."

"Right."

"Beer?"

"Sure." Tony went into the kitchen and returned with two bottles of beer. "Your place is nice." I said that last time floated through her head.

Tony studied her. Opened her beer. They each focused on sipping at the bottles. Carrie wondered why she was drinking so quickly. She also wondered if her eyes were so pried open that they resembled a bug. They were on the couch. She couldn't help herself. Carrie threw herself at him. He was taken by surprise, but he let it all happen. When they pulled themselves apart, Carrie sat back on the sofa and went off. Her eyes were doing that bug thing again, she knew it. She was up. "I'm sorry, Tony, I just realized, I need to turn the iron off. Big job interview tomorrow." She didn't get up though. She stared out in front of her. Tony investigated his beer bottle. He was letting this play out. Carrie bit a fingernail. She fell into herself. Tony waited, watched her. Carrie stared out in front of her. A normally talkative person reduced to grave silence. She berated herself.

"That's fine, Carrie, go and do what you have to do. And good luck on the job interview." He didn't ask her what it was for, nor did he inquire into her suddenly sullen turn of mood. She looked good to him, and the kiss was enervating. He walked her to the door. "Another time, Carrie."

"Sure, Tony... I'm..."

"Don't think about it. I'm glad you stopped by." She smiled and was sure it was going to send splintery lines across her face; and then the cracks would follow and the disintegration.

She got back inside her place, almost slid down the door again, but refrained from doing it. Carrie lit a candle and placed it on the coffee table. She saw bats flying through her head. She put her hand over the lit candle and let the flame torch her palm. Then she put the other hand up over the flame and did the same thing. Falling into the couch, Carrie began to weep and wail. Reduced to ashes. Out on the fire escape now. She looked down. A cold gust nearly lifted her off her feet. *And, I'm gone,* she thought. A glorious feeling for a moment. She came back in and knocked lightly on Bubby's door. He was up reading a comic book. "Mom, is everything all right?"

"Sure, Bub, everything's fine."

Bubby held his tongue.

"We're looking at more houses this weekend." She stared into the room. Bubby swallowed. "We'll finally get that dream house of ours. Just wait and see." Bubby didn't care about the house. Even if half his life – mostly school – was bathed in misery of seven kinds, he wanted to stay put. He felt sympathy for this woman. There was no way for him to help her. The winds of derangement were going to blow her into its vortex.

"Yes, Mom."

She closed the door.

The next day, Tony opened his blinds. Nothing but blue skies. As he was brewing his coffee, his mind turned to Carrie Welter. How much could he put up with just to screw her? Would he be the one to ease that pressure? He knew he wasn't up for the task. But then, her scent, the way her hair fell over her breasts. The temptation to give in to her was strong. If it went bad. A short walk from his comfortable existence to insanity. He was able now to see things from different vantages. He poured a cup and imagined his letter to his daughter winging its way toward her. Would she be there to receive it? Was it the right address? He had to have faith now. A covenant in the US Mail, belief in her being there to pluck it from the mailbox.

He waited for a rap on his door. A woman banging. Tony shook it off. His mind was conjuring her up, his desire rising, that fuse being lit. He pictured her son, Bubby, a boy lost in the shuffle, the tangled mind of his mother. He felt for that boy. Just trying to hold his ground in the maelstrom.

Tony dressed and put his camera in his bag. Out in the hall. He wanted to meet her and didn't want to see her at the same time. Should he knock? Just to let her know he was still interested. Down the stairs and out the front door. The air was crisp. Meandering down Que, left on 14th street. He took a photo of a check cashing place. Then one of a mortuary. The math problem disjointed in his mind. Chasing money, ending up in a box anyway, needing money to pay for the box. Windfall, more checks cashed, more caskets picked out, winning, fool proof enterprises. A completely windless day. A photo hung on a pole of a fallen teen, not killed in canon fire, but in warfare just the same. Tony doesn't take a picture of the boy. He does snap off two more of a bodega. A woman in a fur coat (fake?) passed. She was wobbling on high heels, one of which was broken off. He longed to photograph her. But he kept his pledge. She clomped down the street. The woman starring in a narrative unspooling in his head. He saw her out on a frigid night, lost and hurt and stuck. Tony walked down the hill. Picture of a bail bonds shop. Another of a store with metal grating over the windows. Trapped. This is what circumstances, bad luck, the city, has done to people. It has squeezed. Tony promised himself to buy a better camera, one to replace this piece of junk.

Bubby lay in his bed writhing in irritation and impatience. He got up and stared out the window at the building across the alley. His naked body felt alien to him. He put on sweatpants and a t shirt and left his room. The apartment was quiet. Stomping elephant like, he made his way into the kitchen. He took large bites from a block of cheese, not bothering to cut it into pieces. He stared up into the cabinets. The pill bottles had names on them that he couldn't decipher. Perhaps, some of them took her up, while others took the edge off. He stared at the one in his hand. He shook the bottle, then replaced it on the shelf.

She's with Swanson, Bubby thought. At first, it made him queasy, but when he started to ponder it, it began to give him pleasure. Isn't that what she needed? And the thoughts of the house out in the suburbs. He couldn't criticize her. He looked out the kitchen window. Redson's pimpled face popped into his mind. Bubby went into his room and lay down on his bed. He became aware of his rapid heartbeat. Western Civ teacher. Assistant Principal. Legs in stockings crossed. None of it worked. Tomorrow. The meeting with Redson at Stone. Integal, irony, iron, jack it. He wondered if there was a dictionary in this house. The ripples across the ceiling. It was a beam hitting him in the head. *Oh, crud.* He turned on the bedside light and stared up into the bulb. On another stretch of road there was a boy with the same dilemma. He too had to choose between doing the right thing and doing something dangerous. What can that boy say to Bubby? He lay there as the numbers on the clock flipped over. A clang when one turned. Abe's face. *He's going to let me have it. Or worse, he'll never want to come within five feet of me ever again.*

Bubby picked up the comic book that was lying on the nightstand. He willed the virus into his cells, urged his blood to receive the bacteria. He'd stay in the whole day. It would be a plan, but it wouldn't make him feel safer or more comfortable. Syphilis, Tonsilitis, Giardia. He threw the covers off him and rose to a sitting position. Then down again. He fell asleep eventually and, in that slumber, he was safe.

The clock radio blared soul music. *Cause when we kiss, ooh, fire.* The first thing he mumbled to himself, after he grunted, was Fuuuuuck! He sat up on his bed. A new pimple had sprouted on his chin. It had company. No doubt from the pressure and stress. He had no other recourse but to head out to the bathroom and go through the motions of grooming. The water beat down on him. God was in the shower head, eyeing him, waving his finger, blaming him, admonishing him, judging him. He went to work on a few of the whiteheads. One spurted its goop on the mirror. He brushed his hair and teeth. His face looked different; his eyes faraway. The apartment was quiet. He saw there was a twenty on the breakfast table. Bubby eyed it. Blood money. His mother came out of her room. She had bags under her eyes. "Go up to the burger joint for lunch, Bub. On me. Treat Abraham. Bring me the change. No. Well if you have any." A wave spread through him. *This is what I'm doing today, Mom. I'm sticking up a grocery store with this kid named Redson.*

Carrie went through the cabinets. Bubby couldn't feel his left leg. She uncapped bottles, laid out pills, filled a glass and gobbled them down. At least she was still taking them. "Going to be a great day," she said. Her words spilled out of her. "I've got plans, Bub. I'm taking an economics class." She froze as if she'd forgotten not only what she was going to say, but herself in its entirety. "We'll get that house." Her face drooped. Bubby, with his own problems, wasn't able to analyze her or provide any comfort. Bubby finished his cereal and stared into the living room. His left leg was still numb. "Mom, I, uh…"

"What is it, Bub?" Carrie was flipping through the newspaper. Bubby's eyes fixed on the words, Triple Homicide. The story was on the back page of Metro and was incredibly short considering the barbarism it related. There was no photo. Bubby was lying in chalk, gunned down by the store owner, never to breathe another breath again.

"I'm…"

"Spit it out."

He rubbed his leg to try and bring it back to life.

"I'm not, you know, feeling…"

She had her eyes on the want ads. Now she was ripping out half the page.

"You look fine."

"I, uh…"

Bubby went into his room to retrieve his backpack. He heard his mother slam a cabinet. It made a louder sound than it should have. He said goodbye to her on his way out the door, then looked back into the living room and all the comforts it provided. He met Swanson in the hallway. The older man had a backpack slung across his jacket. "Hey Bubby."

"Hi, Mr. Swanson?" Tony looked squarely in Bubby's eyes, paining him.

"Have a good day up at Carter."

He knows all of it.

The eyes again. They cut right through Bubby's heart. Bubby wasn't sure he wanted to walk down the three floors with this man. He was soldered to the floor. "Forgot a book," Bubby said. He went back into his apartment and told his mother he had to use the bathroom. He sat on the toilet while his insides ate themselves up, chewed them to pieces. *I have nowhere to go.* Carrie was slamming cabinets again. Bubby went out and looked at her. He had his own problems. Her face was hard. Bubby knew there was a place, not far away even, where none of this was happening. If only he could be jetted there.

Abe studied his friend out there on the street. The kid knew all about it and Bubby couldn't escape his friend's glare. Only one sentence was spoken on the boys' way to school, and it was said by Abe. The school was rising on the hill when Abe spit it out. "It's never too late to pull back, Bub." They went their separate ways once inside the double doors. Lindsey Shapiro, who normally wouldn't look in Bubby's direction, let alone speak to him, did.

"Dangerous forays? New developments?" Bubby moved past her. He sat through all his classes, his guts turning. The teachers droned. Bubby was deposited on the street after. Stone was there, rolling through the trees and grass. Redson wasn't there yet. Integal, irony, iron, jack it. He turned the word integal into integrity and crumpled. Abe's eyes, Swanson's investigative glare. He paced the workout station by the creek. And then the water came up in a big wave. It was enveloping him, washing him and the whole neighborhood away with it. He was carried away on the wave, flailing and trying to scream, with none of his words heard by anybody.

He saw Redson approaching. Down the hill, with this stupid, arrogant look on his face. He was dealing with his own fear in his own way. Then he was upon Bubby. They didn't say anything. Redson looked about him, then unzipped his backpack. There it was. The iron. He passed it to Bubby. It was small, but strangely heavier than he thought it would be. A quiver of anticipation rushed up from his gut to his throat. He raised the gun up and down in his hand. Electric.

"We'll take the bus," Redson said. He took the gun back from Bubby and dropped it in the backpack. "You'll work the door. When the place is empty, you'll stand out there and say the place is closed for repairs, or lunch, you decide. While I'll be inside cleaning them out." Bubby couldn't produce thought, but his emotions were about to make him explode. They got on the bus. Bubby was a hologram. He longed for that place where none of this was happening. Wondered if Redson was as scared shitless as he was. I, uh, forgot something at home. My, uh, stomach isn't right. My mom is, uh, expecting me...

They clomped off the bus. Redson moved with purpose. Bubby was three steps behind the kid, a thousand cameras shooting his every motion. Through his own nervousness, he knew Redson's was an act, the confidence a sham. A shrieking pain in the middle of his shoulder blades. This urge to please, to fit in, to be just like him. Yet, a big part of him knew that this kid was a jerk, if not menacing, that he was headed into a bad fate. Bubby, though, was still following him. He looked around him, even if he couldn't really see anything. The roads were strewn with garbage. Soon the rats would take over the entire city. Run, his guts were telling him. They came to the store. There was meshed wire covering the windows.

"Remember the plan," Devon said. Bubby tried to look his accomplice in the eye, but it was difficult. Fear was gnawing at him. Was it really going to work in the mastermind?

"Yeah," Bubby said. He remembered a cop show. How this criminal had swagger that would match what Redson was surely displaying at that moment.

Devon waited for a few customers to pay up and leave, then he opened the backpack and removed the pistol. Bubby stood in front of the store. His legs were shaking. He didn't hear everything clearly, but was sure he heard Devon say, in a shaky tone, "The register. All of it." A mother with a small child approached the store.

"We're closed, ma'am," he managed to utter. "Come back in ten minutes." What a stammer. She looked at him and saw right into his measly soul.

"You work here?"

Bubby swallowed the filth residing in his throat. "That's right, ma'am." Just like the good cops would say. The woman adjusted the baby on her hip and glared at Bubby.

That's when Bubby began to pee himself. The urge came on so quickly that he had no time to stop it. The woman sniffed. Bubby said, "Ah..." Then tore off. His sense of direction was scrambled. He ran east, then through a park. What he didn't know at the time, was that Devon Redson was also peeing himself as he waved the pistol in the air with a shaking hand. Devon got none of the money in the register. He was off and running, but west. Devon still had some wits about him. The store owner was on the phone with the police. But, halfway through the call he decided not to pursue it. No harm, no foul. Bubby sat on a park bench in his wet pants. All the streetlamps around him started to bend and shake, they reached for him, tickled him, and shone their lights on his exposed body, his shame and ineptitude. The whole city was on top of him. He hadn't gotten any relief from the fear yet. The urine had leaked into his shoe. It went squish. He got up and ran north, then turned and headed west. He couldn't find the road back home. Then he remembered the twenty his mother had given him. He uncrumpled it and smoothed it out. Then he inspected his pants. A fat line of his pee, the stench ripped open the humiliation. He had never seen this on TV. He made his way to the road and tentatively waved down a taxi. He sat behind the driver so as not to expose his peed-on pants. Then he watched the city unfurl out the window. All the trees, their branches, the trash bags, the stoops, the people smoking and trudging into the dusk, everything, was laughing at him. Halfway home, he saw him. Devon was running. Was it? *Yes,* Bubby thought. Devon had wet himself, too. Two babies trying to enact a man's deed, to live in a grown-up world of crime and danger. *We failed miserably,* Bubby thought, and that thought brought a smile to his face.

Please let her either be out or in her room. No Swanson or Nilsen in the stairwell. He found his keys. No sign of her. He peeled off his jeans and shoved them under all the other clothes in the hamper. Then he jumped in the shower.

Carrie entered. She had bundles under her arms, and once inside, she plopped them on the floor. She stood amidst all her purchases. It was a sea of items. Hard to imagine her hauling them upstairs in one go. For a second, she wasn't able to move away from the pile. Her face spasmed and then set itself in stone. The cabinets were bare of all medicine. She found one tranquilizer lying loose on the shelf. After inspecting it, to make sure it was the right one, the one she needed just then, she popped it in her mouth and swallowed it down with a sip of water. Then she straightened her skirt and took a deep breath. She glanced at the window and the fire escape, ran her hands over the oven knobs. She thought of her father's face that one day. Trying to approach him with a problem of hers yet met with a hard stare and an unwelcoming pose. *In the ground*, she told herself. He was now lying in dirt. She lifted the window up and shimmied out onto the fire escape. She looked down and saw a cat with a mouse in its mouth. Carrie clapped and whooped. Three stories down, enough.

Bubby went into his room and looked into the full-length mirror. He became sickened. Glad it was over, though. What kind of a way is this to go through life? He pictured Redson's wetted pants. Something grew in the boy just then. Not joy exactly. More like glee. He got dressed and braved his mother. The bags were still sitting there slumped on the living room floor. One of the plastic bags shifted and Bubby heard its movement clearly. She was just standing there, not able to say anything to her son. "Mom?"

"Oh, Bub."

"What did you buy?"

She went into a flurry. Pulling clothes out of bags, laying them on the sofa, holding some up to her body for her son. Bubby could care less about the items of clothing; what got to him was the look on her face. For a moment, he saw it. He took a step toward her but was knocked back suddenly by her look.

"Oh, a ton," she said. "Just look at it." She was almost in despair. "Here's a shirt for you." It was a hideous teal golf shirt. They'd rip him apart if he showed up in school in that thing.

"Mom, I, uh, did something..." She was in a frenzy and for a moment it caused him to forget everything that had happened that afternoon.

She didn't hear him. A two-step bind. Each of them in their corners bloodied but enmeshed still. Trapped, but no fight would ensue. There was five feet separating them. It could have been a desert. "Me and this kid. You probably don't know him..." His mother bit her lip. She didn't care about the bags. She moved past Bubby on her way toward her room. Bubby was left standing there lost. He looked into the bags without seeing any of the things. He put the TV on and lay there. False comfort. He thought of making things right with Abe, telling him he was done with Redson. But hadn't he already sung that song? He had to set the record straight. Abe was too good a friend. The phone felt hot for some reason. Bubby put it down. Paced, then picked it up again. Abe's Mom was effusive as always.

"Sure, Bubby, I'll get him."

Bubby twirled the phone cord around his fingers while he

fidgeted. He heard Abe breathing into the phone. Bubby's legs did that numb, disappearing act again.

"Abe?"

"What?"

"So, you're there?"

"This is my voice, isn't it?"

Bubby made a fist with his free hand. The line went dead.

"And? Did you pull off the big caper?" Bubby wasn't going to tell the gruesome details. The whole of it must have been about to run rampant through the school. You couldn't get anything past them.

"No, I, uh… ran at the last minute." His voice went into a chirp. "I didn't do it!"

"Happy fricking congratulations."

Left leg gone in the wind. Line silent again.

"This is your second strike, Bub."

"I'm cutting the cord with Redson."

"Find God, repent? All that good stuff, Bub?"

"You've got to believe me, Abe. It's over." Silence.

"I've got to go and do something that doesn't involve teaming up with louts and knocking over grocery stores."

Daggers.

Quiet. "So, are we good?"

A pause. "Yeah, I guess."

"Don't be like that Abe. I screwed up. And now I'm trying to fix it."

"See you in the morning. I wish you luck in facing the whole school."

Pricks to his heart.

Bubby put down the phone feeling worse than he did when he made the call.

His mother came charging out of her room. She had a new outfit on. Bubby couldn't say if it suited her but said it did anyway. Her velocity threw him. Instead of trying to keep up with her, he lay on the couch and flicked aimlessly through the channels on the set. An ad for a knife that easily cut right through a tin can, a courtroom where small claims were settled, a guy who could make a bomb out of the most basic items. He sat there as she whirled and hissed around him. "I'm running out to the pharmacy, Bub. Do you need cream for that rash?"

His words came out in a soup. "No, I'm good." She maneuvered her way through the shopping bags and went out the door. "Aren't you going to…?" He looked at the bags. His mother had no idea that Bubby had spoken.

Abe's words rang in his head. Facing the school. He already felt the eyes on him. Bubby got his jacket on and went down to Stone. The dark clouds, the trees, the creek itself were laughing at him. He was moving toward the water, but it felt as if he were standing still. All kinds of excuses and scenarios started lining up in Bubby's head. Any way to avoid that box of a building and all the eyes on all the bodies moving down its hallways.

He started walking South toward the lower bridge that spanned the Parkway. There'd be a spot where he could land where cars weren't flying by. He wouldn't die; he didn't want to end it, but it would break enough bones to keep him out of commission for a while. He got up to the railing and peered down. Four floors, maybe five. Left leg doing that disappearing act again. He climbed up on the railing. All the people in the cars were going to appointments, heading toward concerts, movies, a home cooked meal. The wind swept through him. He wobbled for a moment, then fell back on the sidewalk. A couple walking by took him in, more derision than sympathy.

Bubby crumpled and started walking west toward his apartment. *Can't even get that right.* The word *tomorrow* crept up into his brain. May it stay away, should it never come. He found himself at Abe's house. He stared into the window to try and gauge what mood his friend was in. He ascended the stairs and waved his finger over the doorbell. He couldn't bring himself to ring. He walked home to find his mother on the landing between their place and Tony Swanson's. Again, his problems covered up any kind of consideration or wonder he could muster up. Carrie Welter had a guilty and excited look on her face. Bubby didn't register this, nor did he care.

"Just a little visit," she said. "There's food in the fridge." She went to knock on his door.

"Mom, I, uh…"

"What, Bub?"

He hung his head.

"Nothing."

She came up and squeezed his cheek, a little too hard, like he was still a baby. The light dimmed in Bubby's head. When he got inside, he told himself to come up with something, anything to keep him away from school the next day. The right ailment to fake, and in that fakery, he would be spared.

Chapter 4

Tony studied her as she lay sleeping, and snoring lightly, beside him. He saw the child in her, the girl pushing outwards. A turn, and he was sent somewhere. An empty space, then pictures of the past. Then, their lovemaking of a few hours before. It was there, gone, back in new clothing. She was uninhibited, charged in her desire and he did his best to keep up with her. It had been a long while since he'd experienced the things she did to him and the way she did them. Now she was conked out. He got up and rearranged some of his photos. Each one calling up words and ideas. He brought a photo of a used car lot up to his eyes and studied it. There were flags strewn across and through the place. Furloughed dreams attempting to be renewed. Scraping for the bread. This is what he wrote on the pad after he had glued the photo to it. He looked carefully at six or seven more photos, made notes, then went back into the bedroom. To his surprise, Carrie Welter was sitting upright in bed smoking a cigarette. She was on the verge of exclaiming something.

"I'm just thinking, Tony."

"Oh, yeah?"

"We'll have a lot of space in the 'burbs." *Go on, Carrie,* she thought. *Buy the house.* She studied the cherry on her cigarette. "Why don't you come out and live with Bub and me?" The words tumbled out of her mouth. He cocked his head. A feeling of revulsion rose up in him. It surprised him, and for a moment he was at pains to quell it.

The look on her face told him to proceed with caution. He sat on the bed. "That's just not possible, Carrie. I have my whole life here." A clock in the woman, ticking louder and stronger. One little tip away.

"I've got plans, Tony. Things are going to take off now." She put her bra on. What was he to her? Some kind of branch to cling onto as she shot through the rapids. "Watch it all unfold. I'm on top. No one can knock me off this mountain. Come with me."

Then her face drooped. She dared to look up at him. It may have reminded her of her youth, of trying to look up into the eyes of, at that time, the most important man in her life. This notion was buried deep down inside, untouchable, unknowable to her. Now she was awash in the man's fortune, and she had no idea how that was helping her. She'd spring for something for Bub, buy Tony something too. That would set her free, yet Carrie felt like a punished child. She couldn't bring herself to say anything else. That curtain had gone down over her eyes once again.

Bubby woke at three a.m., startled, urging a self-induced, fake fever. There'd be no way to shake this malaise. He got up and went into the living room. All the shopping bags still lay on the floor. He piled them into the corner of the room just past the TV. A thought struck him. He went to the cabinets and found the tranquilizers, read the label, then downed five of them. Nothing but a lightness, then sleep.

Bubby and his mother both slept past noon. She didn't even notice that he was still in the apartment. It was only when she heard a sneeze that she rushed into his room and declaimed, "Bub, what's going on? Are you sick?"

He turned it on. "Yeah, feverish. Feeling lousy." She entered the room. Abe's face filled up Bubby's mind. Judgment passed. "Can't go to school."

"Too late for that now." In her hands, fists. "Okay, then, get some rest, honey."

Carrie went to the phone to call the realtor. She rubbed the phone against her face and imagined the steps that had to be taken to secure that first house they looked at. The woman answered. It was still available. Carrie looked at all the shopping bags and then took a quick glance at her current dwelling place. An odd memory intruded. Her mother dragging her to the place of worship, the look of utter discontent on her face as she was pulled along. Then alive to this: *A time to laugh a time to weep.* "Are you there, Mrs. Welter?" Being dragged to the suburbs against her will.

"Yes. Just thinking. I'm looking at a few more places in Camotop."

"Well, I can arrange another viewing on that Seneca place. Would you like to see it this Saturday?"

What I'd like to do is overdose on pills and booze, then take a nosedive off the fire escape. "Yes," she said weakly. "Saturday will work."

"How about two?"

I'll be history by then. Non-existent. Ashes. "Two. Fantastic," she managed to utter. She hung up and went to the cabinets. The bottle of tranquilizers was light. She stared blankly into the bottle then lost it. She stormed into Bubby's room and launched a tirade.

"First of all." She stopped. Then she threw his legs off the bed, and he fell onto the floor. "You're despicable, you know that. No good for anything. You do nothing around here. You just hold on to the remote control like it was an appendage." She halted for a moment and that curtain came down. "You went into my medicine." Bubby was still lying on the floor.

"No, never. I wouldn't." There was that line the detective used. Everybody lies. Some of them are bigger whoppers than others, though. *I pissed myself on a botched robbery* filtered through his brain, *and everyone at school knows it.*

"You're a sucky liar," she yelled this. "Get dressed, you can still make 5th period." Her voice shrill. "Look at you. Things have to change around here. This will not do." She was still shouting. She ran her hands through her hair making it stick up in all directions. He usually pitied her, but now he was afraid of her, scared of what she might be capable of doing. She went to him and tried to lift him up by the armpits, but he was too heavy. Then she kicked him in the stomach. The blow shocked both. Next came a weaker kick to his shins. "Get your shit together, Brandon. Now!" Bubby flinched at the sound of his given name, the one on his birth certificate. He flared up, then sank back into that fugue. She stared at her son who was struggling to get up, the sedatives still going to work on his nervous system. He still needed a way out of going to school. Carrie fumbled with her cigarette pack. Her hands were shaking as she lit the butt. After a few drags, she went to the window, opened it, and threw the cigarette out. Bubby pictured it spinning and falling end over end, then landing in the alley only to ignite a blaze. He rooted for that fire.

Carrie had eased off. "We're going back to see that first house we looked at. This Saturday."

Bubby stared at his mother. What was going to happen now?

"Get dressed and get your ass to school." She left the room and began going through all the shopping bags again. When Bubby got out into the living room, fully dressed, he saw that all of them were tipped over and that some of the clothes were spilling out all over the floor.

Bubby slung his backpack over his shoulders and braved the front door. He saw some bills on the kitchen table and grabbed a twenty. Tony came out of his apartment.

"Home for lunch, Bubby?" He had on his pea coat and held his bag in his hand.

"Yeah, wanted a home cooked meal."

They went down the stairs together, all the while Bubby thinking that this guy was giving it to his mother.

Once outside, Tony headed east on Que, while Bubby went north on 27th, knowing full well he had no intention of going near Carter. He wondered if Redson was in the building. He doubted it. Bubby turned and looked up at their place. He pictured his mother lighting her hair on fire with a cigarette, her running through their streets like a maniac. He turned on Pine, then circled back on 28th street. There was no relief. Each step. Every nip at his heart, the embarrassment and shame trickling through his pants just like the warm urine on that infamous day. Hope arose. He moved with a lighter step. Maybe there was a way out of this after all.

He opened the door and stepped into Scott's, the tranquilizers still making his tongue fuzzy. He ate a sub at a corner table. Arranging it. Not even having to go into the pee incident. The sub started to taste better.

Up at school rumors flew. They busted in and ripped the place off. A girl came up to Abe at his locker and told him his friend was some cool cat, going in there like that and pulling off the caper. Redson was being praised for his part as the mastermind. Would all the talk reach the ears of the principal? The hallways were all abuzz. They each held guns, they knocked it over and carried fistfuls of money out of the place. No mention of the fear, the peeing in the pants, the shameful escape. Redson walked the halls clothing his devilishness in purity. He was up high in the clouds, almost felt like he was flying up above all the kids in the hallways.

Bubby bought a pack of cigarettes and walked down to the jungle gyms by the softball field. He took one out and struck a match. It burned so he put it out. By this time school would be letting out. He sucked his gut in and walked back to his place. No Nilsen, No Swanson. His mother was out on the fire escape staring off into space. She had that faraway look in her eyes. Nothing registering in her line of vision. The pity, again, was tamped down by his own difficulties. He couldn't go to her. He didn't know how, had no idea of what he could say. He went into his room and put on a pair of sweatpants and a T shirt, then he got in bed and slept off the rest of the sedatives.

Tony was making his way through a northwestern neighborhood, his bag slung across his body. He walked and tried to get into that transparent, enlightened state, knowing full well the difficulties that implied. His footsteps registered and with that and his breathing, he tried to blot out his thoughts. How Ashley was lost, his life leading up to this point had been a series of humiliations. After all those thoughts were dispensed with, he found a groove again. All the nagging left him. He took a picture of a well-kept tennis court and a Maple tree, bare and wanting. Then a hulking brownstone. A clean and spacious park. *Don't think, record*. A school that welcomed only these affluent kids. The fire station, the fighters always responding in a timely fashion. A restaurant.

Food arriving on time. The façade of another brownstone, *don't they have their own problems, too, inside there?*

He walked down 34th Street and made a left on Massey. The shops glittered. Thoughts of Ashley again, she alone out there without anyone to turn to. Or worse, her living a sordid life. It made him want to throw the camera on the ground and smash it to pieces. The look on Carrie's face. The hopelessness of all endeavors. The muck we all sloshed through.

The sun dove down. He could see the river down below. Songs made about this land. He whistled one of them. Cars scuttled across the bridge. Home to booze and pills and broken promises. It all was about to crush him to pulp. He had to put one foot down in front of the other, though. The bridge was above his head now. There were eating establishments down here, less garbage strewn about as there was the other day in the eastern part of town. The coffee he bought from a vendor soothed his aching head. Trying to piece together his thoughts, soothe his mind. And, all these props, the people, scurrying and hurrying, all the buzzing. He'd had enough of this now. He made his way back up the hill and walked east.

Carrie was on the phone shouting. "I was promised a place in the class. This is beyond the. I need to talk to your supervisor. You're doing me wrong. It's all just an injustice." She was rising higher and higher. Bubby woke to the tail end of her outburst. He had come back "after school" and had collapsed on the bed. He put his head under his pillow and dreamed of being alone on that train car, just him and the sound of the wheels grinding on the track. *Where do I buy tickets, how do I pick a destination?* He cursed himself and his mind latched on to yesterday, the warm urine running down his leg. *I got it from her*, came into his mind. She shouted on about being taken. He wanted to kill her just then. Just go in there and end her. He squeezed the pillow over his ears. Her rant would never come to an end. He got up and looked out the window. The woman across the way was vacuuming. Bubby pictured her naked, her boobs jiggling. This warmed him. She was sweeping the cleaner across the floor with her hips going la-la-la. He longed for her to turn around so he could see her ass. He put his hand down inside his pants, but got nowhere with it, his mother's tirade from the other room blocking out all thoughts of eroticism.

Bubby stumbled into the living room. His mother might have smoke coming out of her ears and nose. He froze in her presence. There were bills splayed on the coffee table. Bubby was about to reach down when his mother started her engines. "Don't even think about it, Bub." Her face was about to crack. She went on in a voluminous tone about one disgrace and injustice after another. Bubby didn't feel the need to confess anymore. He wondered where Abe was just then. Oh yeah, he was at Taekwondo. Kicking some real ass. The bills were about to be picked up in a breeze and scattered through the apartment. "What?"

"I didn't say anything."

"I can see your eyes, pal."

"No."

She fell onto the couch. "What are we going to do?"
The pity rose again, then Bubby became confused and silent.

"This is no..." She put her hands up to her face and started bawling. Bubby could only wait it out. She lifted two twenties in the air. "Take it." Bubby froze. He knew where this was heading, and indeed when he went for the money, Carrie pulled the bills back toward her chest. "You've got to earn it. From what I see, you're just..." Bubby couldn't look at her. He pictured that seat on the train again whisking him away to a newer, fresher, better place. He forced himself to look up. His mother was frozen stiff, her face about to splinter. *What words could I use?* Bubby thought. He felt sorry for her again.

He tried something. "Why don't you go across the hall?"

Her face melted somewhat, and her emotions began to shift. "What do you know about that?"

"No, nothing. I just assumed."

Carrie dipped her head and cradled her face. Bubby looked out the window and dreamed. A squall was coming in. It would blow all this away. Lifted, sent flying. There'd be some sort of reckoning. "Don't assume, kid." Kid? She'd never called him that before. "Stick to your lane."

Bubby was about to say, "Mom, please." But he couldn't produce, nor imagine producing those words. The space he occupied on the sofa was an island, his mother standing there on one of her own. He wanted to feel sore from the kicks and punches she'd given him. But he felt nothing. "We'll see the house on Saturday. It'll be good. Maybe we'll get it. Start new."

Carrie's hand shook as she tried to light her cigarette. Bubby stared into the black, lifeless TV screen. He pictured the landlord in the comedy, the cop in the drama, the teacher in front of his multicultural class, none of them had good words for him. His mother raced down the hall toward her bedroom, wailing all the while. "This won't do. It won't goddamn do." She slammed the door. The brutality of the sound caused Bubby to flinch and then the fear came. She would do it. He saw it so clearly. And then?

Bubby went into his room and pictured the looks from the other kids at school. He looked up at his ceiling and made a pact with himself. *Get in there tomorrow and face the music.* He picked up the novel he was supposed to be reading for English. *What did the killing of a bird have to do with this story?* His eyes went blurry after a few paragraphs, so he put the book down. The clock laughed at him. It was deathly still. He crept down the hallway and stood in front of his mother's closed bedroom door. He could hear her sobbing. The crying took on a new dimension: deeper, thicker, more penetrating. Hand in the air, knuckles ready. Slinking away from her crying jag.

He put his shoes and jacket on and made his way past Swanson's door down the stairs. The streets melted on his way down to Abe's. He was pulling himself through the sludge, his head barely peeking out from the muck. The clothes he wore were covered with mud and Abe's were spared. The house sat there in all its majesty and pride. Bubby rang the bell. Abe's mother, as always, was glad to see Bubby. She ushered him into the foyer and called for her son. Abe got to the door. He had that judgmental look on his face. Again, he saw right through his friend. "Hey."

"Hey, Abe." Abe came out and they sat on the stoop. He stared at the cars going by on 27th. A small group of people were gathering outside the Baptist church, no doubt on a break from the AA meeting they were attending. They milled around, smoking, drinking from Styrofoam cups, then they slowly began to form a circle. Bubby followed his eyes.

"You wouldn't believe the developments at Carter."

Bubby had to swallow. "Developments?"

"Yeah, you and fuck face are heroes."

Bubby's heartbeat quickened.

"Turns out they caught wind of your exploits. They think you two have balls." Abe spit. "Do you have balls, Bub?" Bubby felt the warm urine escaping his member that day and sluicing through his jeans.

"I don't have a horse in the race… anymore."

"You nimrod. What does that mean?"

"I've parted ways with Redson."

"You skipped school because you were ashamed of it all."

"Abe. Listen."

"Grow some integrity."

Bubby was slammed in the chest by a blunt object. He couldn't begin to respond.

"You're up there," Abe said. "The both of you. Up on this pedestal now."

"I…never meant to."

"Yeah, yeah. Sing your song, Bub."

"No, I mean. Are we good?"

"Yeah, I guess so." Abe got up and put his hand on the doorknob that would lead him into his house.

"Abe?" Bubby was going against his mind. "I'm going to try and be better." He felt small and large, and only Abe could bring that out in him.

"Wait until you're carried around the halls tomorrow like some victorious gladiator."

"No, see, it didn't go down like you think…"

Abe studied his friend. The look was searing. Then Bubby watched Abe go into his house. He didn't look back and Bubby was left there socked by the door that was slamming in his face.

Chapter 5

Carrie did her dance. Should she go over, wouldn't it be better to stay put? She lit cigarette after cigarette, all the while going back and forth in her head. It brought on thoughts of her youth. Impulsive, then lost in indecision, back again. Hovering outside her father's study afraid to go in and disturb the man.

Now, as she paced, her thoughts started to get fuzzy. She couldn't get a grasp on any of them. Digging and digging, about to fall into the hole. *This won't stand,* she thought. Another cigarette, hands still shaking. She went to the cabinets and swallowed two pills. She was about to take off. It was a particular sort of Carrie Welter tailspin, and she couldn't stop it. She lifted the window up and got out on the fire escape, looked down, felt the crush of her bones for a minute, then eased herself back into the apartment.

The effects kicked in. The contents of the pills sliding into her brain cells. How a pill can change the way you think. She went into the bathroom and fixed her hair and used blush to conceal her anger lines. What she saw in the mirror made her want to spit at her reflection. But, on she went.

Tony was in his den going through pictures, adding the occasional thought below them, when the doorbell rang. He raised his head, looked out the window, and sighed. Looking through the peephole, he tried to get a sense of her mood. Sex and disturbance, or avoidance. He let the ringing and banging go on. He tiptoed back to the peephole and made a deal with himself. There was always another day, and if not, there wouldn't be any other days at all. But here she was, right across the hall. His solitude was crushed. He opened the door and greeted a woman who was trying hard to conceal the disruption that was occurring within.

"Tony?" Then she looked down.

"Carrie." She was demure, or at least faking it.

"Can I come in? I've been…"

Tony looked back into his place. A large wave of guilt washed over him, and his lower parts came alive. "I'm afraid this isn't a good time, Carrie."

She looked up. Something sparkled at the corners of her eyes. "No? Well."

"I'm in the middle of working."

You don't take me out. We never do anything. Try any sort of pouting. They weren't there. She dared herself to look at him. Tony was afraid of an outburst. Carrie retreated. In her place, she sat on the couch and buried her hands in her face, her eyes tearing. "Why?" she exclaimed. Bubby was inside his room. He walked to the closed door and took in the sobbing. He was numb. No thoughts entered his head. Bubby rooted for Tony Swanson, that he'd be the one to take her out of the funk, Bubby knowing full well, though, that the funk was the funk and that it was here to stay.

His alarm clock went off at seven thirty the next morning. He stumbled toward his closet, then decided to take a shower. The apartment was cold. He saw that the window in the dining room was open. The fire escape was cold metal. Bubby approached. He was about to lose it. He climbed out there in his underwear scared shitless. Looking down, he didn't see a dead or ailing woman. He shut the window with a slam. His heart was going crazy. He went to her room and stood outside the door. It felt like a long time, him standing there. He cautiously pushed the door open. There was a lady-sized lump under the covers. He closed the door and went into the bathroom to take a shower. The hot water felt enlivening. Then it was the picture of Devon Redson's face in his head, and that of all the other Freshmen at the school.

She still wasn't up by the time Bubby had finished his cereal and placed the bowl in the kitchen sink. He got his backpack on and made his way to the door. No Swanson, No Nilsen, no old lady on one, nobody. On the way to school. Again, the dreams of boarding that train and heading out into the vastness of the west. Wheels shooting sparks in all directions. He hung his head when the school rose in the distance. He had no choice but to enter through the double doors.

Carrie woke up at ten. She went to the bathroom and plucked at her hair. Then a flash. I was out there last night. She shivered, went to the cabinets, and took a tranquilizer. The fridge was empty of everything except for milk and bread. She opened the paper and found herself looking at the ads for used cars. She got up and showered. Brushing her hair, a strange thought came to her. I'm about to lose it all. All the strands of hair are going to come out with every brushstroke. She got dressed, then pulled $10,000 out of the drawer. It was a wad, and it nearly filled up her small purse.

Mr. Scott greeted her. He had that trusty smile on his face. Carrie picked at her eggs, a plan entering her head. It was down on 12th. And it would work perfectly. She got on the bus, feeling like saying to all the other passengers, "What? Haven't you all seen a freak like me before?" Snow was swirling and sinking from the sky as she entered the lot. It was a red '78 Trans Am. She saw tiny, almost imperceptible specks of rust on the wheel walls. But she bought it anyway. $7,500. She filled out the paperwork with a man in a bad mood. The money was hard to part with at first, but hand it over she did. She got the keys, and this rush of endorphins nearly knocked her over. A minute later, she was wheeling the car out of the lot. She jerked down 12th, trying to get used to the clutch. After a while, she was passing other cars, in and out of traffic. She got to Canal, disobeying the speed limit. Nothing could take away the rush she was feeling.

On the highway, then out River down to Seneca, driving way too fast. The power, the feeling of invincibility. She could drive out to West Virginia, fast, crossing rivers and scaling mountain roads, and never look back. I'll make one room an artist's studio, the basement a place for Bub to listen to records and entertain his friends. Then her eyes bulged. She clasped her hands together, in her mouth deposits of bile. *Never. It won't happen.* She wheeled the car back toward the highway, this time driving even faster and more recklessly. At one point she was in the oncoming lane. No heed to cops, an accident, her demise. "This is the last time you fuck with Carrie Welter." She put on the rock station. *I tell you what's wrong before I get off the floor.* She was back on Canal, this time heading east. She stopped off at a liquor store, got a bag with her purchase and got back in the red dandy. Back to the city, sipping at the beer. In and out of traffic, passing cars left and right. No need to ever leave this vehicle. She parked in front of their building, shut off the engine and leaned her head back, took a sip of beer, then crushed the empty can into a sliver of tin. *I'll show you. I'll prove it to all you bastards.*

Bubby couldn't take the way everyone was looking at him. Shapiro was smiling and trying to get up close to him. *I peed myself on that caper and so did Redson.* He was navigating a sea of peering eyes. Abe came up to him between classes, eyes dead serious, and said, "You happy?" No, Bubby wasn't happy. He wanted to run from the place. Redson approached at lunch. His eyes had that mischievous glow.

"Let's plan another one, Bub."

"Don't you remember what happened on the last one?" Redson couldn't be stopped nor suppressed nor put in his place. It took all of Bubby's willpower to turn away from him. The eyes in the cafeteria were all searching and admiring. That's the kid, their eyes said. Right over there. He knocked over a store, fearless, and then ran with all this loot. Bubby wanted to know where all this courage and loot were stored.

Abe knew, of course he knew. They walked home together. "You shits for brains botched it, didn't you?" A flame lit up Bubby's insides. He couldn't hold back.

"Yeah, Abe, we botched it. We ran chicken shit out of the place."

"There it is. Redson failed as the big mastermind, didn't he?"

"We both p…" He couldn't say it, he'd never say it.

Abe got up to his door and looked back down at his friend.

Bubby entered a place where courage and honesty went to die. This he could barely take. "It'll blow over, Abe, and things will be like they were. I told you. I'm done with the kid."

"If I had a nickel for every broken promise," Abe said, then he disappeared into his house.

Carrie was bolting left and right through the apartment when

Bubby put his key in the lock and entered. He thought he would need something to tie her down. The place was clouded with smoke and Bubby almost had trouble parting the plumes nor keep breathing. Was something burning on the stove? He watched her scramble and talk, then go to the window in the dining room that led out to the fire escape and jam it open.

"Big things are happening Bub. There's this light out there and we're going to step out into it." She returned to the living room which gladdened Bubby. He could only gape from the eye of the storm. *Won't we get scorched?* He thought. "Are you with me?" She took a drag of the cigarette then mushed it, half smoked, into the tray. Bubby looked at the ashtray and saw many half-smoked cigarette butts crammed in there. If smoking was a sport, she wouldn't win any competitions. His first thought was to go over and get Swanson, that maybe the guy could knock some sense into his mother. Bubby had seen her like this before. He told himself that it would blow over. It was just a matter of letting it run its course. "The house is ours." It wasn't. "We're going to turn it into something cozy and special. We're off on an adventure. No, no, keep your coat on. I want to show you something." Bubby couldn't move. She went into her bedroom and grabbed the keys off the dresser. She moved back into the living room with purpose. Bubby noticed that the shopping bags were still on the floor, only that they had been squeezed into the corner of the room. His heart sank, but he tried to ride his mother's wave of possibly dangerous joy.

She put her coat on, and they exited the apartment. She stopped and glanced at Swanson's place, then hurriedly descended the stairs. Carrie led them to the Trans Am. Bubby stood there and swallowed. He was both thrilled and terrified. "Isn't she a beauty?"

"Did you? ... I mean. Buy this thing?"

"I did. It's for the both of us. Once you get your license, you'll be able to drive it." Bubby's first thought was that she had stolen it (jacked it). Then he was filled with excitement. They got in. Carrie started the engine, and they heard it roar. Then she pulled out on Que. She jerked the beast along the street, and they zoomed off to the east. The engine roared. It nearly lifted Bubby off his seat. She drove the speed limit, but once she had made a left on 16th, she opened her up. Bubby's excitement was so awash in fear. They were both going to die in a car wreck. She'd wrap this red monster around a telephone pole and that would be it. Bubby held tightly to the arm rest on the door. "Got some pep, eh, Bub?" They passed all the houses of worship lined up on the road and Bubby recited some hacked up Bible references in his head. I am Job, I go along, God, I don't have a clue as to why you're doing this to me; Jonah, get out of the fish and take a breath, look around, swallow it. Traffic lights, then the military hospital and a stretch of dense woods, then out into the open. She ran a red light and Bubby gasped. His fear was a living beast looking for a way to exit the cage of his body.

He couldn't help it. "Mom!"

"Oh, Bub. Don't worry your pretty little head." She managed to light a cigarette. "Just seeing what this baby can do."

"Still. Don't you think...?"

She opened it up further. The speed threw Bubby's head back against the headrest. He was sure he'd never been so afraid in his life. When he heard the sirens from behind, he was almost relieved. Carrie slowed, then looked into the rearview. She pulled off to the side of the road and took a deep breath. She hadn't registered the car yet and knew she was in for it if she got pulled over. The police car sped past them, on to bigger prey, and Carrie exhaled. She made a U-turn and drove the rest of the way back home 10 miles an hour under the speed limit. Bubby dared himself to look over at her. He couldn't deny it: through the fear and anger and sadness, rose this feeling of love. It was there and then it disappeared, he didn't investigate it further.

She took a pill when they got home. Bubby wondered if this was harming her further, or if it was part of the cure. She got out on the fire escape and commenced to chain smoking. Bubby lay on the couch watching a rerun of a sitcom. He didn't laugh when he was supposed to. The phone rang. He got up and lumbered to it, surprised to hear the voice of Lindsey Shapiro on the other end of the line.

"Bubby? Hi. Lindsey? Lindsey Shapiro. How are you, Bub?"

Pins in his chest. "I'm good." He looked toward the fire escape.

"Can I see you? I'm just so in awe."

A rodent was scurrying through him looking for specks of food.

"See me?"

"How about after school tomorrow?"

"Yeah, I don't know. Sure, after school tomorrow." He forced himself to say more, but he couldn't think of anything worthwhile.

"Big Bubby. Scott's? 4."

"Scott's, 4."

"Sleep tight, big man."

Bubby put the phone down. Again, the feeling of the pee leaking through his pants. Then he went to the living room window and stared down. The red car, the rolling coffin, still sat parked on Que. He wanted to throw up.

In bed he couldn't keep from imagining Lindsey Shapiro's ass in his hands. There was so much to squeeze, to grab onto. He was about to lose it right there in his bed. His mind and body were shooting him off in all directions. He heard the door open and his mother leaving the apartment. He waited a few minutes then made his way to the cabinets, paused for a second, pill bottle in his hand, then opened it and shimmied a pill out of it and downed it with a glass of water. Bubby looked out on the fire escape and saw Lindsey Shapiro standing on the roof of the opposite building, she was beckoning to him, waving him over, come and get it big guy, I'm waiting here for you, her tits jiggling with her movements. Look what a failed robbery, a pee in your pants fiasco, could get you.

Back in bed a smile opened on his face. It felt like someone else was smiling, that he wasn't capable of that action. He dove in, completed. The bathroom smelled of perfume. He pictured his mother at Swanson's and then some unwelcomed images hit him. Back to Shapiro, he told himself. He washed himself, then realized the pill was going to work on him. Bubby stumbled back to his bedroom and collapsed; all his thoughts driven away by the little white pill. His dreams were scattered and vivid and embarrassing. Walking the halls of Carter, Tyson coming up to him and saying, "You know, Welter, you're only wearing socks." Bubby looking down at his flimsy excuse for a member, on display for all, the socks, waking up in a spasm. At one point he woke in the night with the urge to seek out his mother, to find something he was lacking, to receive some comfort, even if it was false. He didn't do it.

At school the next day, Bubby walked through a million admiring smiles. His feet were an inch off the ground, while his insides were torn to shreds. Redson had his head held high and seemed to be reveling in the looks of the students more than Bubby was. That sharp gleam in the kid's eyes. It flashed. Bubby wondered if Jefferson, his math teacher, had caught on to the rumors. As Bubby sat there in the back corner of the room, he pictured the intercom cackling to life. "Pep rally at four," it would say. "Yearbook committee at four thirty. Oh, and we'd like to send a word out to our two heroes, Devon and Bubby, who, against all odds, knocked over a grocery store, only to escape with a bag of money. Way to go guys. Keep up the good work." The bell rang and Bubby was deposited into the hallway. Redson came up and winked at him. "Stone Creek Friday, Bub. Let's keep this thing rolling. Bust 'em up. Take no prisoners." Bubby looked into Redson's eyes and saw something there that freaked him out. He wanted to run away. Go flying out of the building, run along streets and in an alleyway put on his cape.

"Don't you realize, Devon... That we... pissed...?"

"What?"

"All talk, no action, eh, Bub?"

Bubby slinked away. A kid two heads taller than him, Paul something or other, patted Bubby on the back. Bubby went into the bathroom. Two students in there threw their cigarettes out the window, afraid Bubby was a teacher. He got in a stall and sat on the toilet, his hands propping up his chin.

Bubby got to Scott's early, but Shapiro was already sitting in there at a booth. Bubby couldn't feel his legs and wasn't sure he could make it the twenty steps to where she sat. She waved effusively. Bubby sat down. Shapiro flashed a grin. She stared into Bubby. Scott came over and took their order, Bubby asked for a grilled cheese, knowing full well that he wouldn't be able to take a bite of it.

"Tell me all about it," she said.

Bubby's heart was a bruised knuckle slamming into his ribcage. He pictured Abe's face. "Nothing much to tell."

"Oh, come on, Mr. Modest."

Bubby's eyes went into a spasm. He was looking all around him, not seeing a thing. All he could think of was the four o'clock show, of getting lost in the rays of the tube, the stupid plot of the sitcom. "It was well planned. We got in and got out."

"How did it feel to hold that gun?"

Scott came over with their food. Bubby knew if he took a bite, he would begin to crap himself.

"It was all right."

"Come on, Bubby."

"I don't like to talk about it." Warm pee.

Lindsey was beaming. She got up off the booth bench and leaned over to kiss Bubby on the cheek. This set him off. The windows of the place turned red, green, blue, and yellow, then back to red, before becoming translucent. All the things out the window began to melt. The lampposts, the trees, the people even. He wanted to run. She talked about different things for a while. Bubby got Scott to wrap his sandwich up. When he returned with the wrapped food, Bubby was sure the man gave him a look of warning and judgment. Here's your sandwich, he'd say, you no good, lying coward. Lindsey gave him another kiss on the cheek at the corner.

Bubby was greeted with a cyclone when he returned home. All his problems drifted away when he took in the state of his mother.

When she ran down the hall and went into her room, his problems resurfaced. He couldn't lay on the couch, nor turn on the TV. The pills were replenished in their little green bottle with the white top. Bubby read the name of the medicine and then the description of what the pills were supposed to take care of. He opened the bottle and removed one pill, then a second, downed them together with a chug of water. The bags were still in the corner of the room. Bubby thought about his grandfather. The way the man would stare at him, never try to have a conversation, or engage with him. Bubby hated him for his mother. In a way it was fitting that he was dead.

Bubby went over to the bags of clothes and stood over them. The money it took to get these clothes. The Trans Am parked outside, the money that had poured into his mother's hands. It all made Bubby ecstatic for a moment. But that feeling died when he looked down at the clothes in the bags. Carrie came racing out of her room. She had a million plans and wasn't afraid to voice a few of them. "I'm going to open a café. Right down the street, Bub. Gourmet coffee from all over the world. Books on the shelves lined up neatly against the walls. Or I'll buy that parking lot down on Pugh and turn it into a row of shops. Boutiques, a record shop. Oh, you could hang out there." She stood there in the middle of the room and froze. She went into silent mode. Bubby waited. Her eyes weren't dancing any more. Bubby had one eye on his own problems and the other on his overwrought mother. Carrie went into the kitchen and opened the cabinet. Bubby heard the pill bottle opening, then the faucet running. *That would slow her down.* She came back into the living room with a wad of bills in her hand. She peeled off a few twenties and held them out to her son. "This will get you something nice." Then she pulled the bills back a few inches. Bubby waited. This little game. Finally, she passed them over, a glazed look in her eyes. "Buy something for yourself." Bubby took the bills. *These are tainted.*

"Mom," he would say, "I tried to knock over a liquor store, but peed in my pants and ran down the street like a disgraced fugitive, and now everyone at my school thinks I'm this big man on campus."

She came out of the kitchen, her engine still humming about to overheat. She looked around the room. Bubby could lift her, scoop her out of this. Was it his job? She began going through bank statements, exclaiming all the while. Bubby the spectator to all her wildness. She became immersed in the papers. "I'm going to do some Spanish and Social Studies homework, Mom." Are you okay, he could have said? His mother didn't look up.

He worked on the Spanish, finally getting the difference between *ser* and *estar*. Then Shapiro entered his thoughts. He had his head buried in her ass. He delved in; finished. Lying there, then back to the novel for English. He still thought it was a bad title, that it didn't fit with what was written in it. He went out to find his mother smoking and fiddling with the stereo. Ten seconds later the music was playing... *I'm just a soul whose intentions are good, oh Lord, please don't let me be misunderstood.* Bubby watched her. His thoughts melted away, along with his problems. Genuinely concerned for the well-being of his mother. He took her in from behind. Something loosened within him. Munched at a cuticle on his index finger. *Should I just assume that she'll be all right? Will that make her all right?*

"Mom? Are you all right," he wanted to say.

"Sure, Bub," she would say. "Everything is hunky dory."

Everything is so not hunky dory, he told himself. "Mom," He uttered this word audibly. The next were just in his head. "I tried to knock over a grocery store and wound up peeing myself. Now all the kids at school think I'm this big hero, but it's all a lie. We screwed it all up. I'm a fraud, I have no integrity just like Abe says."

Later things began to calm. Bubby was watching the show about the crime stoppers with the van, the guy with the mohawk. He could smell the perfume his mother was spraying on herself in the bathroom. She came out in a blue dress with a wide, red belt around her waist. "Just going across the hall." This made Bubby happy. After she left, he was bombarded by the trail of perfume she left in her wake. This pleased him too.

Tony looked her up and down, then into her eyes. He didn't like what he saw there. He had a beer in his hand but wasn't sure if he should offer her one. She busted into the apartment and then froze in the living room. She looked around haphazardly. Carrie was making plans in her head. Then Tony came up behind her and said this wasn't the best time. He looked at the way she was dressed, and the word, expectations, filled his head. *How can I dismiss her,* he thought, *would it set her off?* She turned and threw herself at him. Kissing and hugging and holding on. He took a step back to ease things off. She glued her head to his chest. "Oh, Daddy. La, la, love me." She mumbled. An incomprehensible slush. He gently pried her loose. She spoke into his chest. "Don't do this, Tony. Don't throw me away." He looked toward his office. The project was stalling. He was faltering. There was no time for this. A show was starting at the 15 Minute Club in a half an hour. He had promised a friend he'd be there to meet him. Carrie's eyes were marbles clinking this way and that. "I'm trash to you. Just someone to babysit. Well, I know when I'm not wanted."

Tony remained quiet. He tried to make his glance as soft as possible. But, inside his head he couldn't stop words, such as, hate, despise and revile from popping up to the surface.

"Use me, then kick me to the curb."

"Carrie. Just try and calm down."

"Now you're giving me orders?" She looked down at her pumps. "Don't I look good?"

"You look great."

"Then, take me."

These words quieted things. "I've got plans. I need to be someplace."

Her eyes bugged out. She stared at everything and nothing in the apartment at the same time. "We'll go out. See a movie. Someday?" she said.

Tony was quiet. If he made a sudden move, he'd be stuck with this woman living ten feet from his own place. "Sure, Carrie. But now, I've got to be going."

That tormented look returned to Carrie's face. It caused Tony to take a step back. He wanted to comfort her and toss her out of there both at the same time. With his outstretched arm he ushered her to the door. "This dress. Look at it. It's gone to waste. I did it for you."

"You look great, it's just."

"Right. You have no time for me. Well good riddance to you Swanson." But she didn't move. She hovered. No idea what she was waiting for. "We're done." Her head dipped. Then she found her legs and made it to the door. After she was gone, Tony stood there gaping, wondering what had just happened.

The next day, Bubby made the walk down the path toward Stone Creek. The sky, with the low sun hanging in it, was trying to tell him something. *Go the straight and narrow.* He thought about Lindsey and the kiss she gave him still plastered to his cheek. Bubby thought of Abe and his rock-like bearing. He'd do this for him, not for Lindsey, and not for Redson. He wanted to be his own source of authority. Remove himself from the evil constraints of Redson. Bubby felt enlivened and realized it was resolve oozing in. He looked at the buildings surrounding the park; they were swaying and winking at him. He knew what Redson wanted to drag him into. But was he a friend? Bubby shook his head, right down by the creek, and said out loud, "No, no, no." His mother was shooting off in all directions. Bubby imagined a few bad outcomes but was hazy on the details. The creek was about to flood again.

Redson came barreling down the hill. He had that confident look on his face, yet Bubby knew his dirty secret. He'd peed himself on the robbery, too. "Got here early, Welter. I like the determination." Bubby felt torn up, yet there was this kernel of courage plugged in his gut. Redson spoke fast. It was another grocery store up behind the school and to the east. He'd get the pieces again. He'd lead them in. After that he wanted to hit the Moselys' again. Kathy would be none the wiser seeing how much time had gone by. Bubby saw the mole on Kathy's chin, the softness of her eyes. After he stopped talking, Bubby looked down at his shoes then out across the park. A dog was running wild across the field chasing some imaginary ball with the utmost freedom.

There are certain moments that grow so large. They make clear thinking difficult. But Bubby dug in deep. "I'm out, Devon."

Devon locked eyes with Bubby. For a second, he thought about giving in, agreeing to take part. "Out? There is no out."

Devon ran his hand through his hair. He was trying to organize his play. He turned away from Bubby and looked up at the bridge. "I need you, Bub. Come on, this is the big one. We'll be rich."

Bubby felt a surge. "We both know what happened on the last go around. You pissed yourself and so did I."

A fake smile from Redson. Incredulous. Embarrassed. Still pushing. "I need you, Bub."

Bubby felt shot. Streams of electricity coursing through him. "You're on your own, Devon. I'm out. Done." This last word was the most demonstrative of all the other ones. Bubby started to walk away.

"I'll tell them," Devon said. "That you pussied out."

Bubby wanted to turn back, but he kept walking. Away.

Bubby and Abe were sitting on the stoop. The AA meeting was having its break and people were milling around smoking and holding Styrofoam cups. Finally, they formed the circle. Bubby's future unfurled in his head. It came on so strong. He too would be milling about outside an addiction meeting, trying to figure out where to get the next drink, the next pill, faking it long enough to get his due, then ditching every principle laid out in the meetings. But he would be inside the circle. Abe was quiet. He was watching the traffic move down 27th Street. "Redson wants to do another one," Bubby said.

"And?"

Bubby stuck a finger inside his sneaker and began scratching. "I told him I was out."

Abe looked up, then at his friend. "For once and for all?"

"Yeah."

"Oh yeah."

"The kid could ruin me."

Abe got up and paced the sidewalk. "Stick to your guns, Bub."

Right there and then. In his mind, Bubby had already told his friend about the warm urine flowing down his jeans. That he was a yes man, a coward, and a liar. "There's something I haven't told anyone about that day at the grocery store." Abe came and stood over Bubby waiting. "I pissed myself and ran off like a frightened deer." The words hung in the air. Abe looked off down the busy street.

"There it is then," Abe said.

"There it is."

Abe snorted out a laugh, then came back to himself and the moment they were in. "That took some balls."

"My secret's safe with you?"

"You know it."

"And you believe me when I say that I'm out?"

"Yeah."

"And behind me when Redson comes after me. When he tries to ruin me?"

"I'm a blue belt in Taekwondo. Long from the pinnacle, but still."

The boys began laughing. A delivery truck with blue and orange lettering on its sides screeched by. Once it passed, the neighborhood settled into itself. Bubby got up and headed home, thoughts of Kathy Mosely and how Redson was already on the lookout for a number two man. Those eyes of the poor girl.

The apartment was empty and eerily quiet when Bubby returned. He looked out the window. The Trans Am was nowhere in sight. Bubby put his bag down and went in and poured himself a glass of milk. He took down the pill bottle and shook it, put it back in its rightful place. She was driving the car into a telephone pole; he'd get the call any minute now. In the living room, he made up his mind. He started picking up the shopping bags, one by one, and bringing them down to his mother's bedroom. When he was done with that, he had to decide where he should put all the items. He began folding sweaters, pants, dresses, scarves on the bed. Not sure where she would want them, which dresser drawer to put them in, he just made them as neat as he could and laid them on the bed. After this was done, he picked up that same novel he was meant to read for school, and found himself weirdly drawn in. The TV sat there waiting for its turn, sad at the inactivity.

Meanwhile, Carrie was behind the wheel of the Trans Am, careening down Route 1 on the Virginia side. She stopped at the park and watched the planes fly in overhead. Then she got back in the car and began stomping her fists on the steering wheel. "Damn it!" She said. "Screw it all!" It was past nine. Carrie opened it up as she got near the cemetery. She hadn't registered the car, yet, but this fact didn't slow her down. Her insides were percolating. More. More speed. More. More danger. If she felt like she had a soul, then that was disintegrating. She drove slower over the bridge as the city closed in on her. She could go no further. Arriving home. As she locked the doors, a black carpet enclosed her. She could barely make it the fifty steps to the building. She couldn't think about anything that wasn't dark and forbidding.

Bubby was in his room. She poured herself a tall glass of whiskey and drank it down in three gulps. The view outside the window in the kitchen made her sad. All the shit of the city rising up, taking her down. Everything was sad, their situation, the hope the money would bring them. Stuck. She shimmied herself out on the fire escape and tossed the glass over the edge. It hung in mid-air then smashed on the concrete. Carrie clapped. The black turned to green for a moment. She was enlivened, but out of herself still.

She sat at the dining room table. No wherewithal to write a note. She got the bottle of pills. The words flowed through her head: *I'm trash, you're kicking me to the curb.* Carrie, I just don't have time for this now. Her father's hard glare, mother nowhere to be found. The black carpet again. Pen and paper in front of her. She couldn't even figure out what words to write down. And this is it. *I gave it a shot,* maybe? She dumped the pills out on the table. Two by two, then three by three, four by four until they were all gone. Had to have been at least fifty. She twirled herself in the living room. Dizziness nearly put her on the floor. She had enough wits about her to put a song on. *We are living in a material world. And I am a material girl.* Then she took a nosedive onto the living room carpet. Blackness had returned.

Bubby went out for a glass of water around midnight. He had already been sleeping so he was in a stupor, but not enough of one not to notice his mother crumpled and passed out on the floor. "Mom!" He found the bottle of pills on the kitchen table. "Mom! What did you do?" Perhaps he had rehearsed this very incident. He went to her and shook her, shouted at her. He put his hand to her neck. He was sure he felt a faint pulse. Then he found the phone. They were there in their red uniforms in less than twenty minutes. Later, this would surprise Bubby. The two paramedics were calm. "She overdosed." Bubby handed one of them the empty bottle. They got her on a stretcher.

"Who else is here?"

"Just the two of us."

"You can ride with us." Bubby hurriedly got dressed and followed them down the stairs, his mother lifeless on the stretcher. "Wake up, Mom! Wake up!" The ambulance moved down the city streets slower than Bubby would have imagined necessary. When they got inside the hospital, a nurse said he'd have to wait outside while they wheeled her into the ICU.

"Make any calls you need to, son. Father, whomever." *Father?*

Once his mother was wheeled away, Bubby got caught up in all the what ifs. He looked through the little window in the door. He was shot numb again, his world tumbling down. He sat down and cried in the waiting room. *And now it's going to be over.* Hands covering his eyes. Tears streaming down his face. There was no end to the salty streams. *Who could I call? Abe? Swanson?* He just sat there looking straight ahead, his insides turned to mush. Doctors and nurses were moving back and forth at a hurried pace. And Bubby felt his future fold in on itself. All he could do was stare out in front of him. Lost.

Part 2 – Coping

Chapter 6

It was the smell of cleaning products covering a sweat like odor. If Bubby could come up with another word to describe the ward it would be decay. He was sitting outside on a bench waiting for his mother to get out of group. An attendant shuffled down the hallway and smiled at him as she passed. It had zero glamor or drama. 1978. He was seven and his mother had "gone away." Her same sister, Brandy, had come to stay with him. She had been deposited in their apartment again, now – Brandy to the rescue. Bubby was told little that time and knew even less about the events up to now. She threw out her back, they may have said. Brandy kept him snugly ignorant of the details.

Now, Bubby was scared, and underneath that a strange anger. He began calling up pleasant pictures of his mother. The pretty woman, the caring parent. *But, why?* She had the inheritance. Things were taking a turn for the better. She joked with Bubby. They went shopping. She put the cereal boxes in the cupboards. The bills were paid on time. Water coming out of the shower, rays from the TV. She had the misguided motivation to buy the Trans Am, even if it could have been the instrument of her demise. Bubby leaned on his elbows. He'd fight them. The tears wouldn't be allowed to come.

Brandy was outside. She wanted Bubby to have time with his mother alone. Bubby looked down the long hallway. This is the perilous avenue. It's down there in one of those rooms waiting.

The attendant who had passed by before returned. She stopped in front of Bubby. "May I sit down for a moment, Mr. Welter?" Never had he been called Mr. by anyone.

Bubby straightened up. "It's Bubby?"

"What an unusual name. Is it a nickname?"

Bubby looked back down the hall. He pictured zombies coming down, on the march. How could he outrun them? "No, ma'am." He saw no ring on her fingers. "I mean, Ms." She smiled. "Bubby is my name." Bubby knew that on his birth certificate his first name was Brandon. He had never used it and didn't plan to. He was sure he was named after Brandy. A gender twist on naming. Nobody had ever made it clear, though, neither Brandy nor his mother.

"Well, Bubby, you'll be able to see your mom in a few minutes. She's excited to see you."

Are there scars? Tubes running in and out of her body. Wires hooked up to machines. He was glad he'd been home that night the previous week, thanked whomever for taking him out of his room to get a glass of water. "Could she have... I mean?"

"The surgery went well. She's lost a bit of weight. That should correct itself. Physically she's doing well. We have some work to do on her psychic state. Oh look." She patted Bubby's thigh. "Here she comes."

You don't know what you've got till it's *almost* gone. She was way down the hall, puttering. He almost couldn't make her out. It was going to take her a half a year to get to where Bubby was sitting, or at least it felt that way to Bubby. His impulse was to run, put the whole hospital in the rear-view mirror. Smash something. Spit on somebody. Her. The attendant and her thigh patting insincerity. Why was this happening? God had some wicked sense of humor. Belted to the bench. Then somehow finding himself rising. The distance between them was still enormous. The pee was running down his leg, Stone Creek was flooded by an urban tsunami, Lindsey Shapiro was taking back her kiss, all the potholes in the city were simultaneously cratering and everything was falling into them. Still, she was 25 yards away, Abe was dying of some ailment, Swanson was cleaning out their apartment, Brandy scored crack and was lighting up in her car, the whole universe had flipped end over end, who knew what this meant for him, or everyone else inhabiting this planet.

There she was arms weakly outstretched. Bubby looked at her eyes and didn't like what he saw. He also couldn't stand the outfit she was wearing, hospital gown, hospital pants. A uniform used in some bizarre sport that nobody played anymore. He ate his tongue.

"Bubby, my boy." The words barely made their way out through the fog. She gave him a hug and he fought it.

"Hey Mom."

She put her hands up to his cheeks and rubbed. He couldn't find anything when he looked into her eyes. What did he want to find?

"How are you? Brandy treating you all right?"

"Yeah, it's fine."

"I'll be out of here in no time."

"Why can't you just leave now? You look fine," he lied.

"Oh, Bub."

Carrie sat down next to him. "What happened in the house isn't going to happen again. You have my word." Bubby wondered how much medicine they had been putting in her. Scenes from that film popped in his head. The nurse, her goons, deadened patients, enforced insanity -- whose freedom? What freedom? The Chief, his silence, escape. Lobotomy. He didn't register her promise. He wanted to grab her and lead her out of this place. "Be nice to Brandy."

The attendant smiled at them. Carrie bent down into herself. Her chin drooped. She had this aura of loss surrounding her. There was nothing that could lift her back up.

Carrie spoke in a soft and repentant voice. What did she have to give penance for? She rallied for her only child. "Give us a few minutes, won't you?" The attendant shuffled away her shoes squeaking on the linoleum. She turned to Bubby. "Your mom is... how can I say this...?" Bubby's thoughts ordinarily would have gone into overdrive, yet now his mind was eerily still. "... fragile."

"I just need to rest for a while. I'll be back home in no time."

"Come back now, then. You look fine."

"Bubby. I've got a ways to go." She folded her hands. He was looking at the defeated version of his mother. The one who stared out in front of her, lost and falling away. "Go in my top drawer in the bedroom. You'll find some cash in there."

"I don't want money." Bubby looked down into his lap. "We can chill at home I mean. Go shopping. Whatever. I don't know."

Carrie looked down the hall. The attendant was returning. Bubby pictured a ring of keys dangling from her belt like a medieval jailer. Carrie kissed Bubby on the cheek then rose. "You're awesome, Bub. Come on Saturday." Then she was being led away. Slowly. 5-yard line, 10, a trudge, then grinding toward their 10, through some doors Touchdown. Bubby felt that poker of anger again. Then he was out in the winter chill watching Brandy flag him down.

Bubby began skipping school. He'd peel a twenty off the bankroll every day, tuck it into his sock drawer and head up to

Carter just to keep up appearances. Was Brandy privy to this? Checked in at homeroom, then headed out the double doors on the west side of the school. It wasn't a foolproof plan, obviously, his other teachers would record his absences. He just couldn't stomach being in the building, sitting there listening to the drivel.

Abe called. Brandy was cutting coupons at the kitchen table. She always talked about improving Bubby's diet and did start slipping baby carrots and asparagus onto his plate next to the pork chops or meatloaf.

"Bub?"

"Hey, Abe."

"What's going on?"

"I just can't be there."

"You know they'll come after you when it goes too long."

"And things at school?"

"Everything has calmed down. Your reputation has fallen back to earth."

"Do they know, I mean, about my mom?"

"Not as far as I know, Bub, and if they do catch wind of it, it wouldn't have been from me."

The hand holding the phone froze up on him.

"Redson tried Mosely again. He got caught. He's in Juvie."

Bubby swallowed. "Did he...?" *Kathy. I'm so sorry.*

"As far as I know, he didn't mention your name." Bubby was relieved and slightly shocked that Redson didn't give him up.

They agreed to meet the next afternoon.

Bubby took a red apple from the fridge, washed it, and then rubbed it against his shirt. Brandy looked up from her clipping. Bubby took an enormous bite out of the apple. "We'll eat in a few."

He didn't know exactly how to talk to her. She didn't get into his business and kept her questions to a minimum. Bubby was grateful in a way. They both silently agreed that peace had to be restored. He just wanted to keep everything quiet and normal. There was too much going on to act out or cause upheaval. Back in his room, later, tossing a hacky sack up to the ceiling and snaring it. The book he was supposed to be reading was lying on the night table laughing at him. He got that old feeling again. *Had my chance. She'll never have me now.* He was sure all the kids at school knew that his mother was a nut, that she was in the looney bin. Bubby grabbed his love handles and groaned. He fell asleep thinking about Shapiro, smiling about her leaning over at Scott's and planting that kiss on his cheek.

He plunged into dream. Attempting to board a bus. Climbing up what looked like was three steps, but which turned into a nearly endless moving stairway. He kept going up the steps, getting nowhere, while more of them appeared. Come on, kid, the driver said. Huffing and puffing, never gaining entrance into the bus. Up, up. He managed to hop down. All the passengers were the same man. They scoped Bubby out through the windows. His face, but on a middle-aged man. Simultaneously, they all lifted their hands, lowered their chins, and said, Hmmm, what are you going to do, silently. "Dad?" Bubby managed to say to the passengers. Now, a long hallway, dim fluorescent lighting, linoleum, Bubby was wearing only his pants. His body had morphed into something lean and powerful. As he moved down the hallway, doors began to open. He didn't stop to peer into them. He reached the end of the hall. Double doors, with slivers of windows on them. Inside were people in thin white cotton shirts. They were milling around haphazardly. Bubby tried the doors. Shoved them. Nothing. Above him a sign lighted up. It said, End of the Line. All the people behind the doors began shouting, End of the Line, over and over. He turned and started running in the direction from which he had come. Tearing down the hallway. Bubby woke. Unbeknownst to him, Brandy too, he had shrieked.

Bubby's homeroom teacher glared at him when he called his name that next day. Janet Yorn, he called, the name after his. Head nearly buried in his locker. Waiting. First period bell. Then out the east side doors. The air was fresh and dewy, and it was getting warmer. He skirted the hill leading down to Stone. The exit a freedom. He tried to make it last the whole day. Scott's was an option, but he couldn't keep going there, or anywhere, more than once a week. He headed east. Buses and taxis whistled past him. It felt good to be on the move. All the walking had slimmed him down somewhat, helped him move more swiftly. The vendor at the stand smiled at him as he passed the sandwich to Bubby.

"Where are you in from?"

"Oklahoma."

He passed Bubby his change. "Don't miss the art gallery down the road. They have a special exhibit. Americana."

"I'll be sure not to."

Bubby sat down on a bench and unwrapped his sandwich. He took a tentative bite. Eating slower, plus all the walking he was doing, besides slimming him down, was making him more alert. A picture of his mother popped up in his head. He couldn't help but imagining the scene in there. That it was the walking dead. What was she eating? Who was she talking to? How was she filling her days? Which pills were they pumping into her? Maybe he'd ask her on Saturday. A bus stopped at the light, and he read the ad on its side. Are you swamped in debt? Help is on the way. When the traffic light changed, he was able to read another ad on the opposite side of the road. Legal troubles? Call Barney Wright, Attorney at Law. Bubby figured that one day he would have reason to call both. He almost took a pad and pencil from his backpack.

He'd done this before. You were anonymous in the library. The rows and rows of books. A quiet that he could roam around in. He looked about. Maybe there was a Carter field trip down here. He didn't see anyone he knew. There was a shelf filled with magazines. Bubby selected a *National Geographic* and a *Smithsonian*. The magazines under his arm, he made his way to a corner of the stacks and took a seat. For the first fifteen minutes he felt antsy, guilty, and lonely. *I should be in school. This is going to majorly screw up my record.* After those fifteen minutes had passed, he got into a groove. Slowly turning the pages of the *National Geographic* over, taking in the pictures of the Kalahari Bushmen, the peoples of Siberia, a hunt ongoing in Antarctica for the largest jellyfish ever recorded on film. Mesmerized. All these intrepid photographers.

He was coming to the end of the magazine, but wanted to savor every page, each image. Turning the pages ever so slowly. His mother left his thoughts. This happened as he whiled away his days of skipping school. Her face would pop up in his head and then he would summarily push it away. Even the frame of her lying on the kitchen floor overdosed and comatose and gone from this world. What about life without her? Could it have been easier if she had been ushered permanently out of this world? The guilt would redirect his thoughts. Regret would show its hand, and then this feeling he couldn't knock away. *I love her and I don't want anything bad to happen to her. She's doing the best she can with what has been given her.*

Bubby got up to get a drink of water from the fountain. A group of kids had streamed into the library. They must have been about eleven or twelve and were making a racket. They were enjoying the field trip to the library, but seemed to have little interest in reading books, or books in general. Bubby saw himself at that age. He was hanging at the back of the group, his quiet heart beating stronger and stronger. Cautious and aware of how hesitant he was. The Bubby of now trying to put words into the mouth of the younger version of himself. Be excited. Articulate. Enthusiastic. Someone they'd all stare at in awe.

He returned to his seat in the corner. The kids on the field trip were an invading army. Bubby would soon have to beat it out of there. That's when he felt a presence hovering over him.

"Bubby?"

"Mr. Swanson?"

"Tony."

Bubby just stared up. He put the words in the older man's voice box. Why isn't your sorry ass in school?

"Interesting reading material."

Bubby stared down at the magazines. His guilt and shame were now in full view. Even stronger was the shyness.

"I love this place. It's full of gems."

"A little loud now."

Tony laughed. Carrie Welter's condition hung between them. After Bubby made that remark, he slithered back into himself. He'd said too much. "You know, Bubby, I read about this saint once. Dymphna. Seventh Century. She was one of the saints of the mentally ill." Bubby's torso clenched up at the sound of those last words. "She shone a light on those suffering from anxiety, psychic turbulence, and the like. She provided comfort to them. That they are also created in God's image, that we shouldn't ignore them. Embrace the abnormality until it isn't seen as abnormal."

Bubby looked up into Swanson's eyes then quickly away. "Thank you, Mr. Swanson."

"Tony." Bubby was waiting for the question.

"Good to see a young man like yourself here. Even when the world is pressing in upon him." Bubby was pretty sure what he meant but had to process it for a moment. "Anything you need, anything at all, don't hesitate. I'm just right across the hall. I'm thinking about your mom."

Now get yourself back to school.

It never came. Swanson disappeared into the stacks of books while a warm feeling crept through Bubby. He wanted to get up and do something important. Deliver a speech or go outside and do fifty jumping jacks in the park. A smile was dying to break out on his face. Muscles he hadn't used in a while were waiting their turn. He had no one to share his joy with. He walked down E and made a left on 7th. Swanson's kindness infusing his mood. A compliment, a lift. Confidence on its heels. The museum loomed up ahead. Bubby didn't know which way to go when he entered. Too much to take in at once. He found himself sitting down on a bench staring up at these mobiles. Watching them slowly spin, wondering at what breeze was inducing their movement. A girl of about nineteen sat at an adjacent bench with a pad of paper, sketching. Bubby stole glances at her. She was trim with long blonde hair and thick, puffy lips. He was approaching her, all the worries of the world floating away. "Can I see what you're drawing?" She'd turn her body toward his. This open, welcoming pose, all possibilities out there on the table. He had nothing to say about art, though, and he didn't have the guts to approach her, and when he turned toward her again, he realized that it was hopeless. He wandered the halls, checked out the Americana exhibit. Splashes of color on canvass that seemed so basic that it wasn't out of the question that a child could have painted them. He thought there was a certain beauty in their simplicity. Outside. The sunlight burned through him. He still had some money left from the twenty, but he decided to walk home instead. Riding high on the half-life of Swanson's caring words.

It was after five. Bubby still had his lies in order and his backpack on to keep Brandy from sniffing around. He stopped in front of Abe's house and for the first time really took in the place's grandeur. He's centered because of the atmosphere of love and free communication in the house, not by the house alone. Bubby could break down right there on the sidewalk. At his misery, the hopelessness of the situation, his broken mother. Were the street and the lampposts beginning to shake? Was not every car that passed caught in the tumult? A strong wind whipped through and nearly picked Bubby off the street. Where would it deposit him? He held on to the railing that led up to Abe's house. Bubby waited a minute, not a thought passing through his head. He went up the stairs and rang the bell.

Abe's mother smiled. "He's at Taekwondo, Bubby. Would you like to wait for him in here?"

Bubby looked over his shoulder. Nothing came to him. "I can just wait on the stoop."

Abe's mother's facial expression betrayed her. "Sure, no problem."

Bubby's lips parted. He was so close to saying something it almost made his insides burn. He just turned and went out the door. Standing there on the landing. *You idiot.* He trudged down the street and made a right on 27th. His building loomed in the distance. It spoke to him.

He looked up at the squat building, found his window. His mother was circling the living room, hands flying up in the air, and Bubby was there to calm her. The wind picked up again. Bubby was almost shoved into the façade of the building. He got his key out and made his way, slowly, up the stairs, toward Brandy, toward the hole that Carrie Welter made in the place when she was carted away.

Chapter 7

Brandy drove the car slowly down Canal. She had tried to engage Bubby in conversation but got nowhere. She left him in peace. Her jalopy had none of the pep of the Trans-Am. Bubby wondered what had inspired his mom to buy that car. It must have been a symbol of her inner turmoil. Something shiny and sleek and fast to mirror her intermittent feelings of grandiosity at the time. She needed the speed and the gleam. *It was useless now,* he thought, just sitting outside the building. Bubby would leave the building and just stare at the car and think how depressing it was that nobody was taking it for a spin. All that money, and here she was, nearly incarcerated.

He looked out the window in silence, imagining what awaited him at the hospital. He knew that talking would be a good thing just then, but he couldn't bring himself to utter a word to his aunt.

"Look at the trees blossoming, Bub. It looks like snow."

Bubby looked over at her. He raised an eyebrow, but no words escaped his mouth. The road turned into another and before long the hospital was standing there tilting in his direction. Did it give him a slap across the face? His legs surely couldn't operate, wouldn't take him from the car to the entrance to the hospital. "I'll come in and say hello to her, Bub, then I'll wait in the cafeteria." She jammed the car into park. "Be gentle. Well, you know that already."

Bubby was in another world peopled with benevolent strangers. He was moving down the hallway of a new existence. Everyone he met there gave him his due. They showered him with affection, encouragement and kindness. Instead, he found himself getting in the elevator of the hospital and ascending, just him. Where is that other existence? He stepped out tentatively on seven, looked right and left. There was a hole where his heart should have been. "I'm here to see Carrie Welter," he told a woman in a blue outfit.

"You must be Bubby."

Bubby nodded. "Has my mom climbed up on the roof?" He almost said. "Or tried to escape. To run home to me?" Bubby's throat was chalky. The woman led him into a common area. The first thing Bubby noticed was the glassed-in room filled with smoke. He wondered if they were doing experiments in there. Carrie sat on a sofa; her head turned the other way. "Mom?" He was proud of himself for just producing that one word.

She got up slowly as if a great weight was tying her down. "Bubby." She tried to muster the necessary enthusiasm. She put her thin arms around him, and Bubby did his best to return the gesture. Bubby scanned the room. There were the smokers in that glass canister, people sitting around a large table doing puzzles or the crossword, a man sitting in the windowsill staring out at his freedom. Bubby wanted to help that man achieve that freedom. "You look good, son." So do you. No. She had to sit down. Bubby's hands were useless appendages. The stare. He had seen it before. This shield she put up between her and the world. Bubby wanted to snap in front of her eyes. Wake up. "Tell me. Is Brandy treating you all right?"

"She's fine." When are you going to give this up and come home?

Carrie Welter sat not two feet from where her son sat, yet the distance could have been a mile and a half. Bubby watched the man at the windowsill out of the corner of his eye. Was he thinking of throwing himself out the window only to be scraped off the pavement? "Be good to her." The words slid out of her mouth. Wake up, would you? Come to your senses. "And school?"

And school? "It's school." Bubby surprised himself with his sarcasm.

"Bub?" He waited. Then she turned her head and stared off into the distance. He followed her eyes. It was just the big room and all the people being swallowed up within it. "Go easy." He looked at her profile. "On yourself." She turned her head slowly to face him. It took her a while to utter those four words. Bubby was thrown. He didn't know what to say. Left to stare with her at the movement in the room. They turned and sat so that they were facing straight ahead like two strangers sitting side by side on the bus. His thoughts started to rev. Falling off his bike as a kid, her running toward him her arms in the air. A bad grade, a stern reproach. Carrie calling the mother of a kid who had given Bubby a black eye in elementary school. The way that phone call made him cringe.

"When are you coming home?"

"I need to rest, Bub." *From what?* "I wasn't. Well, I just wasn't well. They've got doctors here and ways of helping me get better."

He looked away.

"I read about this saint called Dymphna. She tried to ease the pain of people suffering. Their psychic pain. Maybe you can pray to her."

Carrie moved her lips ever so slowly into a half grin. "You're sweet." She spoke those words crisply. Her hand came up to her son's face. It felt warm. He was in the bathtub, and she was running those hands through his hair, whispering sweet words, and he was awash in comfort.

"I'll be better." He stared into his lap.

"Don't talk like that, Bub. You just keep being who you are."

Carrie got up and started swaying. Bubby stared at a woman at the big table. She was pulling her hair. Carrie took out her cigarettes from the pocket of the outfit. The man on the windowsill had his hand under his chin as if he were about to solve one of the world's greatest mysteries. And this amorphous black cloud descended on Bubby. A thick, dark presence. It was about to take him on a ruthless journey. The End of the Line. The darkness behind those double doors. Never to return to the hallway. Stuck forever in black. He got up and went outside and asked one of the nurses for a cup of water. "Sure, hon." She came back with it. Bubby found himself walking toward the double doors at the end of the corridor. Voices from within. Growling. Barking. Darkness. Bubby peered inside. A few shapes moving around within it. Locked inside there forevermore. The cloud dropped down again. His mind was moving. Jumping from one thought to another, spurred on by sheer fright. He pressed his face against the glass. There were people in there, moving around in circles, a dim light in the corner, a bed with straps across it. Bubby bit his tongue. He'd grab his mother and race her out of there. *She would never wind up in there. Could she, though?* Bubby was about to explode. He turned and walked hurriedly back to the main room.

Brandy was talkative on the drive back to Que. Bubby was happy for the distraction. She spoke about how she and Carrie would steal cigarettes from their mom and walk to the park and smoke them as they leaned against a tree. "Your mom was funny, Bub. Is. She got people's attention. And she was pretty. Is. She got men to turn their heads. You know, it's funny. We had a good relationship and all, but I was kind of jealous of her." Bubby turned to look at her. "Well then she met." Brandy cleared her throat. "Never mind." Bubby knew the story. Or at least the one told to him. He had ditched Carrie and baby Bubby and had headed west. Never a phone call nor a letter. On the tip of his tongue. Tell me his name again. The one they gave him was Felix Welter. That name, and the whole story too, seemed made up to Bubby.

Brandy parked the car and Bubby trudged toward the building. *How do I get to walk around while my mom has to wander around the halls of that place?* The stairs felt like they were never going to end. Brandy was halfway up, Bubby not a quarter of the way. He felt washed out and the black cloud had come down again. All the problems of the world had settled on his shoulders and inserted themselves in the place where his heart was supposed to reside. He stopped on the second-floor landing and looked down, then up. It was the constant rising and descending, up and down, until he couldn't climb and walk down stairs anymore. The building would collapse, and he would still be in the stairwell, right there, frozen on the landing. He had no choice but to ascend.

Swanson's door tempted him. He stopped and peered at it. Swanson's comments in the library lifted Bubby once again. I'm just across the hall. Knock anytime. Apprehension kept him from doing it.

Brandy was already at the stove concocting a meal. It smelled good. All the walking gave him a searing hunger. As they sat eating, two questions formed in Bubby's mind. *One, where is my father? Two, how is it, Brandy, that you are able to be down here taking care of me? Don't you have a life?* He asked neither.

Brandy was talking about hers and his mother's youth again. Bubby laughed at one point, and it caught him off guard less this time. They went to a no nukes rally and wound up chasing these boys around winding up in some strange apartment on the north side of town. And then? She just said, hijinks, youth, innocence. Bubby ate it up.

Abe was shooting baskets at the park. On his way there, Bubby walked past the group of people gathered outside the church smoking and shooting the shit. Bubby was in that circle smoking and sharing his innermost ideas and feelings. Part of something greater than himself like his mother in the common room. A place where he'd have someone to watch over him. A buffer for his wildest sensations. Inside the ring. Welcomed in. In search of that great big pat on the back.

Abe threw the ball over to his friend. Bubby muffed the catch completely, then watched the pill roll away toward the grass behind the basket. He didn't go and fetch it right away. Content just to watch it roll, then settle. Abe gave him a crooked glance. Bubby slowly went after it. He came back and took a shot, but it only collected air and went thud on the asphalt. Abe came up and grabbed the ball with purpose. He took a shot. Nothing but net. After, they sat on the jungle gym.

"They're on to you, Bub."

Bubby looked down. "I know. Maybe Brandy can cover for me. Say it's a rough time."

"Would she go for that?"

Bubby looked toward the church. "I could say she's in rehab."

"Go with the truth."

Those words wouldn't stop ringing in his head until he'd closed his eyes that night and had found himself enveloped in sleep.

Chapter 8

On a normal Sunday, Bubby would sleep well past ten, but today he was wide awake at eight. He looked over at the clock and tried to will sleep back. It didn't work. Brandy was knitting and watching a talk show. Bubby tried to glean what was being said, but it was just white noise. Something about guerrilla warfare, deposing a leader, restoring calm. An ad for a drug came on, side effects, then a Public Service Announcement, neuter your pets, followed by, Be All You Can Be. He scratched beneath his waistband and went into the kitchen.

"You're up early. I can fix us some pancakes."

Bubby came back into the living room. "That would be great."

The racket from the TV filled the apartment. Bubby went and turned it off while his aunt made breakfast. The cackling from the experts faded out and Bubby smiled to himself.

They sat at the table. The boy poured a great lake of syrup on the pancakes and began inhaling them. Brandy told him to slow down. "Can I ask you something, Brandy?"

"Sure, Bub."

"Is she going to be in for a long time?"

She looked at her fork which had snared a bite of pancake. "That's hard to say. Could be weeks, could be months. She's gone untreated for a long time now. And frankly, I'm not sure how she was able to go this long."

"How are you able to stay, then?"

"Don't worry about that, Bub. We're family. Your mom and I have been close for so many years. She would do the same for me. We'll keep everything as harmonious here as we can."

Bubby felt the muscles in his face longing to help him create a smile. He couldn't stop it. It spread across his face. I'm skipping school, he would say. Have been for over two weeks. She wouldn't be surprised nor concerned, she'd look up and say, I've known it all along. It doesn't mean a thing in the long run. You'll right yourself. They sat and ate in peaceful silence.

Bubby changed into sweatpants and a long-sleeved T shirt, looked out the window and saw the tall tree going wild with white blossoms. He wanted to bury himself in the bloom. The sky said rain, but he didn't trust it. His shoes fit his feet like they should. He made his way through the living room – she had the TV back on and had resumed her knitting. Bubby marched past. "Going out."

"Home for dinner?"

"Yeah, what time is that?"

"Let's say six."

"That'll work." Bubby went back into his room and peeled a twenty off the roll. Then he was out the door. He could make it to the city limits if he moved at a brisk pace. Swanson's door was opening. Out walks a threat. He was relieved when he saw the kind smile on Tony's face as he made his way out the door. What Bubby didn't expect was for a girl of about twenty-one or twenty-three or twenty-five to walk out on Tony's heels. No matter how old, she was out of his reach. She had on a jean jacket and her cleavage was well on display. Bubby had to look down, then up quickly to her eyes, sure that he had been outed.

"Bubby."

"Hey Mr., uh, Tony."

"This is my daughter, Ashley." She looked Bubby up and down at a rapid clip. Then she put her hand out and Bubby reluctantly took it. His eyes may have lingered a click too long again. "Ashley's visiting. From Minnesota." Swanson looked at his daughter. "Ashley. This is Bubby."

She looked put out. "Bubby. Some name." Bubby felt small pins going in and out of his organs. He wanted to put his hands all over her, but mostly he wanted to run down the stairs and plunge himself in a gutter. There he went, arms in the air, going down 27th, shrieking and flailing, looking for a hole.

They walked down. Swanson saved him. "We're going to Scott's. Then we're off to Chevie to see the house Ashley, er, we, used to live in. That she grew up in."

"Cool." Ashley looked at Bubby, who was snatching the word back into his mouth.

The air held promise. A soft, welcoming breeze lifted Bubby's prospects. Ashley stared at him. Her eyes were both soft and weaponized. "Come by later, Bubby. I've got a book for you."

Ashley waited impatiently for him to answer. Was she about to stomp a foot?

"Sure, thanks, Mr. Swanson."

"Tony."

"Right."

Ashley hiked her jeans up.

"I'll do that, Tony."

Bubby headed down toward Stone. At the point where city met the green, he dared himself to turn around to catch a glimpse of father and daughter, but mostly to gawk at Ashley. They were gone, though. It was his ordinary street. A city bus whirled by. Bubby turned and descended the hill. He crossed over Stone on a narrow, rickety wooden bridge that needed repair. The woods were dense here. It was difficult to find his footing. Something was pulling at him. There were eyes in the thicket of woods, and they were all telling him that it was of no use, that he should just turn back. Don't go any further. Some huge arm was going to pull him back to Que. He had weights on his legs and arms. At any moment, someone was going to appear. They'd put him in a straitjacket and haul him off. The eyes got bigger. He was naked now. They saw right into him. Should he sit down? It didn't look like it, but Bubby felt like he was staggering. He wondered if it would just be wiser to retreat. Go back to Brandy and the TV and mundane tasks, anything to erase this hopeless feeling.

The way things were lined up, all of it, was skewed.

He stopped walking. A frisbee hung in the air, about to greet a dog's mouth. The disk held aloft for a second then the dog caught it, chomped down on the plastic. A guy was doing pull ups on the apparatus. Bubby looked across the green. More dogs scampering across the grass. A family with a baby on a picnic blanket. Bubby admired the scene. His thoughts came down. He set a goal for himself. Calhoun Bridge and reassess once he got there. His legs were his again. The jungle of Stone Creek Park became a haven. The sky was a magnificent blue umbrella, keeping harmful things away from him. One of the puffy clouds winked at him. He parted briefly from the creek and went up a hill. His lungs were working, keeping time with his legs' movement.

    The bridge loomed up ahead. Underneath was a stall. A

woman was trotting on a black horse around a ring. He got back on street level with all its blaze and bustle. Looking over the railing. It was a long way down. Between the bridge and the ground. He saw Redson's face in his mind's eye. The pee was coming down his leg. But it was removed, all gone, never to come up again. Abe. He kept him straight. He crossed the road and returned to Stone, the woods, then continued north. He kept walking until he made it to the nature center that lay in a clearing, not far from the city limits.

He sat on a rock outside the place and watched people coming in and going out. His legs felt rested. He got up and headed southward.

"Bubby. We need to talk."

Bubby swallowed. His eyes focused on the blemish on Brandy's throat.

"They called from school. You haven't shown up for classes for close to two weeks." Bubby was quiet. He kept his eyes on hers. "I need to go in there with you. We've got to explain what's going on." Brandy wasn't talking down to Bubby and he was grateful for it. She leaned forward in the kitchen chair. "Listen, I know this is tough. Everyone wants the best for you. Tomorrow we're going in to talk to Goldman to get this cleared up. We'll lay it all out. Who knows, maybe you'll get a reprieve."

Bubby pictured his mother in the blackness of the room at the end of the hall. A place you could very well languish in from here to eternity. He found himself nodding at his aunt. The empty feeling slid away from him. His shoulders felt lighter, and he had no desire to sit in front of the TV. Bubby ate the meal hungrily. At one point Brandy urged him to slow down. He shoveled the forkfuls of meat and vegetables into his mouth. Brandy watched him, carefully putting morsels in her own mouth. After dinner, he went into his room and picked up the book. For the first time, the words pulled him in. The girl was about his age, and she had this liveliness and inquisitiveness. It all came together for him. He read for nearly two hours. He still didn't want anything to do with that building and the ants called students marching through it. It reminded him too much of his mother's situation, her imprisonment. He had his walking project. He'd tramp through every corner of this city before he was done.

Brandy was going through her sister's finances. She'd need to access the funds to pay for the hospital stay. Carrie Welter didn't have insurance. Luckily, she didn't need it now. She hadn't worked in over three years. No matter. Funds galore now. Enough to cover the hospital bills, and then some. *You did this at the exact right time, Sister.*

Was the money from his grandfather a peace offering? An apology? A makeup from beyond?

The church was quiet and so was the neighborhood. No clump of addicts outside smoking and commiserating. Abe was quiet for a long time, and it made Bubby nervous. "I don't want to go back," he said.

"Not sure they allow furloughs in high school."

"I'll be sixteen before the end of term. A month to go."

Abe ran his hand through his hair. "And then what?"

Bubby said it under his breath, "I want to find him."

"Finish off the semester."

"I just can't bring myself to go in and sit there like a stone."

"Go until you hit sixteen, then do what you have to do."

Bubby spit on the ground.

"I'm sure you could miss a semester and then resume."

"I feel like the future is nowhere."

"That sounds about right. But we're locked into this now."

Bubby wanted to bring up his mother, but something held him back. "I could appeal to their mercy."

Abe knew what Bub was talking about. He trod carefully. "I know it's hard. Just give them something they can work with."

Abe made Bubby smarter. He helped him think more clearly. He got sentimental for a moment and wanted to say something in that vein. He held back. "Yeah. I think you're right."

"Girlfriends could come in handy," Bubby said. "If we could put that together."

Abe laughed. Bubby described Ashley Swanson in brief detail. Abe just shook his head and got up to return home.

The next day, Goldman heard Bubby out. He gave him two more weeks. In light of his mother's situation. He told him to get all the coursework from his teachers. Bubby went to all his classes that day, fending off stares from his peers. What? Pain in his limbs. He left Carter that day with an armload of notebooks and schoolbooks. There was so much that he could only cram half of it into his backpack. He passed Lindsey Shapiro on the way down the stairs. No mention of the kiss or his mother's condition. She did smile and Bubby's facial muscles did that slight unspooling. For a kid that had gone so long hiding everything, of staring at his feet, he finally felt glad at the fact that he had looked Shapiro in the eye.

Brandy was visiting a friend. Bubby dumped all the books onto his bed. They made an intimidating pile. Then he tied on his sneakers and went out the door. He got caught in the rain on the way over the bridge to the Virginia side. He stopped at the war memorial and took in the soldiers planting the flag. The memorial for the loss is etched in black, shadows. He ran into Swanson at the park by the airport. Planes were sailing by overhead, then wheels scraping the runway. They talked briefly. Swanson had his polaroid around his neck. When they parted, Swanson clapped Bubby on the back and said, "You're looking trim, Bubby. Keep it up." The older man's words, once again, rang cheerfully in his head on his trip back home.

Chapter 9

She was down there. Bubby was looking out the living room window. Brandy was at the supermarket. The Trans Am provided support for Ashley's leaning. Readying herself for a photo shoot. There was so much distance between him and her. She was more than a girl. Bubby was about to let it slip right there. Seductive. That was the word that climbed into that part of his head that produced words. Ashley had on cut-off jeans and a singlet. Her hair hung low and rested on the middle of her back. The car was the perfect prop. She made it her own, was already speeding down the highway on her way to paradise, and Bubby was riding shotgun, going anywhere she and the car would take them. He was about to dive out the window, only to land in pieces on the ground, the words he'd speak to her all garbled. Ashley fixed her hair in the window, threw her purse over her shoulder more snugly, then sashayed off down Que toward who knew what.

Was Ashley privy to the fact that the purchase of this hot rod was the crowning achievement, the last outlandish purchase of Carrie Welter's before she fell? Bubby groaned and went into his room. He saved it all up. Let the urge, the need to expel, be halted, stored for future expulsion. Then he went into his mother's room and started to go through drawers. He found what he was looking for in the top drawer of the dresser that stood in the closet. The clothes in there were lonely, lost without their owner. Bubby had a pang.

He found the bank statements and gulped. It was long. Round and crooked car-loads full of numbers all lined up side by side. Never in his life could he have imagined this sum. He wondered where it all came from. Jess Bagley. Where did he get it all? Once again, his grandfather's face popped up in his head. He got nothing from his imaginative search, and now all this bread. Was it guilt about a transgression? Is that why he left her all this money? Abuse, neglect, two-timing? Bubby couldn't straighten it out in his head. He put the piece of paper back in the drawer.

The phone rang. As if his mother knew what he was doing just then. "Bubby?" She tried to cover up the gloominess. "How are you doing?" But was doing a bad job of it.

Bubby felt caught out. His mind settled on the ward, on the common room, the drifting and lost patients. "When are you coming back?" Bubby wanted to know what crime she had committed.

There was a long pause. She was pulling her hair out. She had her hand over the mouthpiece and was telling some other inmate not to curse at her, she was about to throw herself out the window. "Oh, Bub." She was at the end of the hall, and they'd just let her out to make her last phone call. She was about to burn the whole place down with her cigarette cherry.

"You didn't do anything."

"Did I tell you how well my drawing class is going?" Her words churned out of her.

"No."

She lost her place. Bubby could tell she was doing a bad job of halting the tears. "They're giving me quite a lot of…well, you know."

"Right."

"You're coming on Wednesday, right?"

"Yes."

"Bubby, please, don't hold anything against me."

His soul went to mush. This rotten luck. Bubby picked himself up a few inches and spoke in nearly a whisper. "I don't."

"Be good to Brandy."

Bubby put the phone down and wandered around the apartment for a few minutes. Then he climbed out on the fire escape and pondered the distance between where he stood and the ground below. He gulped back a surge of tears, gripped the railing hard, vowed to be better, to care more, to not have such petty, morose, and self-defeating thoughts. He was leaping over the railing, sailing through the air, waiting for the sweet crushing, and crunching. The place was not the same without her. *Bust her out,* he told himself. Free her. He banged his hand on the railing. When he looked up, he spied the woman in the apartment across the alley. She was raising a hand in the air making it flutter with its movements. Was she calling to him? Come hither young man, I have something for you. He waved to her, and she smiled. Her lips moved, "Don't do it," they said.

He tried to read the novel for English. It was slow going this time. All of its glitter had faded, had something to do with his state of mind. The book wasn't offering him anything. He felt locked out of it. It crossed him up. The pain of feeling stupid, when down deep he knew he wasn't.

As he was opening the fridge there was a knock on the door. Bubby's first reaction was surprise, then the feeling that his privacy was being invaded. Run, jump, flee. This wasn't a mystery seeing that Bubby had been on his own for two weeks now, add to that the fact that his shyness was telling the tale.

Robbed like the failed caper. He closed the fridge and went to the door in a heightened state. It was Goldman. His mother who had escaped. Redson. Shapiro. The boogie man. Going against all his urges he opened the door. Tony Swanson stood there with a book in his hand.

"Mr., uh, Tony."

"Hi, Bubby."

Talk, Bubby. Speak.

A reprieve. "I wanted to give you this." Swanson held the book out to Bubby.

"I, uh." He took it and looked it over. "Thanks, Tony."

"I first read it when I was your age. I found it on my shelves, and I thought of you." The book was in bad shape, which was a good sign, Tony, perhaps others too, hadn't read it, he'd devoured it.

"I'll read it."

Swanson looked Bubby in the eye. "I hope your mother is doing better. Please give her my best."

"I definitely will. I'm going up there on Wednesday."

Swanson put his hand on Bubby's shoulder. "Take care."

Bubby closed the door. There were a few questions he had for Swanson about his daughter but was glad he asked none of them.

Bubby watched Brandy's car pull up. He put on his shoes and raced down to help her with the grocery bags. Bubby knew they had a few things to discuss. His mother's condition, what he was going to do with his break from school. Brandy fought off the pain in her fingers and handed the load to Bubby. Once inside she set to work fixing the meal. Bubby helped with the chopping and mincing. That third person was missing. There was a gap needing filling.

They ate without speaking much. Brandy had this way of reading Bubby. She knew when to hold back and when to induce conversation. Maybe it had always been that way between the two of them. Bubby appreciated it. They agreed that Bubby was to sit at his desk and do schoolwork during school hours. After that he was free to do whatever he chose. Bubby washed the dishes. As he was doing this that black cloud fell on him. He was sure he would never be able to walk or talk again. Afterwards, he went into his room and picked up the book that Swanson had given him. It held his attention for twenty minutes. Then he did twenty-five pushups and sixty crunches.

In the dream he was fighting in a war. He was on a boat in the midst of a swell. The beach was obscured by fog. The gun he held was too heavy for him so that each time he went to lift it up to shoot, he'd drop it from its heft. "Shoot Welter," the soldier beside him kept saying. It was useless, though. He had no strength; he couldn't lift the weapon. "Shoot, man! Pull your weight." Once he finally did get it up in the right position, the gun only went click, click, click, no bullets emitted. He woke up as a projectile came whizzing at him.

All the morning walking had conditioned Bubby to get out of bed early. At seven that next day, he was up doing sit ups and pushups. He moved into the kitchen with a swagger, dropped two pieces of bread into the toaster. He turned around and his mother was sitting at the dining room table. She had a cigarette in her hand and a smile on her face. "Suit up, my boy. We're going shopping."

"All right...!" "I'm making you pancakes, Mom."

"Oh, Bub. You're too kind."

He followed her into the living room and watched her stare down at the street no doubt taking in the Trans Am. Keep her smiling. In the kitchen, as Bubby was taking out all the ingredients, she fed him a prodigious smile that enveloped the boy. There weren't any problems in the place and there never would be. I'll take away all your pain, Mom, so that you'll always be happy. Never will I cause you any grief. You won't ever have to go back. Do you hear me? Carrie Welter was speaking, making plans, but in a calm way. Bubby ate it up. Making pancakes all the while. He flipped, she spoke softly and calmly. She made jokes, he snorted. Pancakes ready. He made a stack on a plate. I'm good and I'll be even better. When he went to give them to her, she was gone. It was just an empty table. Bubby shrank down into himself.

"What's that that smells so good?" Brandy was coming down the hall. Oh. It's just you. They sat. Brandy saw it. "How 'bout we go out to dinner tonight?"

"Sure."

Brandy looked out the window.

"Maybe Abe can come."

"I don't see why not."

They finished up. Brandy did the dishes. Bubby was about to retreat to his room to fulfil the promise he'd made to Goldman. He now had a row of solitary hours of studying lined up in front of him. He could go to the library. Before that he went to the door to get the paper. As he was bending down to pick it up, Swanson's door opened, and Bubby was confronted with the scantily clad visage of Ashley Swanson.

"Heard that was your car down there?"

Bubby stood up straight. She was in a nighty. The lies came

at him, and he could barely contain them nor sort them out. So, he went with this, the truth. "Yep." She took a step closer to Bubby. He recoiled. Her lips were an invitation and the rest of her a threat.

"What say you and I take her for a spin?"

Wait, Bubby said to himself. *I just have to jump off the fire escape.* She smelled fruity. "What's that?" He cleared his throat. Let me just do my homework. That wouldn't entice her in the least.

"A quick little trip around town."

"How'd you know it was ours?"

She threw her hair back. "Just a hunch."

The pain of desire made him want to turn around and go to the kitchen, find the sharpest knife, and slit his wrists with it. Anything to stop the pulsing. Something crawled through him. He was about to bite his lip until it bled. What else could he say? "I'm tied up until eleven forty." Meeting with out of state clients.

Ashley cocked her head and let out a belch of laughter. Brandy came up from behind. "And who is this?"

"Ashley Swanson," she said, now on her best behavior.

"Brandy Fish."

Ashley reached her hand out. "Pleased to meet you, ma'am."

Brandy took a second to run her eyes over Ashley, then said, "I'm off to Upper Marlboro to visit someone."

Bubby stopped himself from disappearing right there in front of the two of them. "It's after eight, Bub. Time to hit the books."

"I'll help you with your math, Bub, like we agreed on," Ashley offered.

We agreed on what now?

Bubby couldn't find his self. It was wandering around the room. He tried to snatch it and put it back where it belonged.

Fighting the desire to annihilate it. "Sure," he croaked.

She receded into the Swanson residence. Bubby needed to slap himself on the cheek. He had to tell Abe about this, but alas, he was stuck in the building on the hill. He retreated to his room and sat down at his desk. The words swam through him without retention, Bill of Rights, freedom of speech and expression, the right to assemble. He tapped his pencil on his forehead. She was naked, right in front of him, and he was having a fit, done, tapped out even before they'd touched. The pain seized him. He did fifty crunches and twenty-five pushups. Even though he had no appetite, he found himself going to the fridge and investigating its contents. He closed the door ever so gently.

The TV was a filthy stranger, a forgotten temptress. Still. On the talk show they were discussing the mental fitness of a guy who had attempted murder. Should we let these people off with a slap on the wrist? Isn't it still the person who did it? Let's not separate the person from his state of mind. The two things are connected. He knew what he was doing because it was his self that did it. A psychologist came on and said that it wasn't the person doing it. It was an altered state. You must separate the person from his illness or temporary state of mind. She didn't know what she was doing, had no control over her mind.

Bubby slammed his fist into his palm. Carrie Welter had something going on that kept her from being herself. A third person had taken over. Bubby saw her sleepwalking in the darkness at the end of the hall. *She'd never raised a hand to me, never threatened me in the least.* And that must go for all if not most of those sitting in that common room. Even the guy who was about to crash through the window where he sat every day, each day, looking for deliverance, for a cessation of his pain. His mother was in psychic pain. He flipped the TV off. Whatever word he wanted to attach to it. She's suffering. Looking out the window in his room, the tears began to well up in his eyes, and soon after the sobs began. He analyzed his crying for a moment, tried to pull himself out of it, then just gave up and let it all rush out of him.

Afterwards, he felt better, cleansed, but weary. The words in the book didn't swim. He began his essay, felt like he needed help, then ignored that notion and plowed on regardless. It was close to ten. He had a twenty-minute break. He was downstairs in sunshine. It broke through the clouds in a blaze. He sat on a bench and took in the rays. Then, he went down to Scott's and purchased an apple and a turkey sandwich. Scott piled it up and gave it to him with his habitual smile. They exchanged a few words. The Orioles' bullpen was looking stronger this year. Lots of live arms. No, Mr. Scott, I haven't been out to the ballpark. See 'ya around, Bub. He was being conservative with the roll of bills. On the bench again, he unwrapped the sandwich and ate it slowly. The car was right there in all its sparkle. Climb aboard, she'd say. We're going on the ride of your life. Math upstairs, a sprinkle of chemistry. The clock ticked away. Would he enact old habits, retreat to sloth?

A knock at the door at eleven forty. Study Hall was a waste, no, a gift. Lunch hour. That gave him an hour and forty-five minutes. He put on jeans and a clean shirt. He paced, wearing out the threads on the carpet. Questions. There came the knock. Bubby felt himself trying to disappear. Right then there was nothing of him, just a bundle of random cells zigzagging around in the apartment. He was on the move. Look out the window. Finger the curtains, try to see. Another knock. The doorknob was hot and weighed nearly twenty-five pounds, but Bubby was turning it.

"Are you free now, Bubby?" She said. Did she wink? "Get all your business taken care of?" She had multitudes in her eyes and the message they gave off scared Bubby. He dared himself to look into them.

"I just have to..." He left her on the doorstep and hurried back to his room to do... what? He looked at his books. Wrote a note to Brandy, then stopped.

"I'm really sorry to hear about your mother," Ashley said from the living room.

Bubby was back. "Thanks," he said as he investigated his sneakers.

A pause. Then Ashley adjusted her blouse. "Where are those keys then?"

Bubby went to the drawers in the dining room and fished them out, instruments leading him to his impending death.

"My mom was the nervous type," Ashley was saying as they went down the stairs. "What are you going to do? You can't blame them." She said it in such a blasé manner that it created this wave of hatred to rise up in Bubby. "She died when I was about your age." Her gaze hardened. Then she moved him down the stairs. Out in the sunshine now. Bubby saw his street in a different light. A layer of gold was covering it. The clouds had this intensity. Reaching himself up he'd grab one and take that ride instead of the one that was before him. Ashley ran her hands over the hood of the car. "Red? What else?" Her shorts were tight, and what they revealed to the boy could topple him. Bubby thought of the last joyride with his mom. The near-death experience. Thrilled and terrified at once. What was going through her head? What goes through anyone's head at any given time? A complete mystery. Bubby was stupefied.

"Where did you come from?"

Ashley looked across the hood of the car. "I've been trying to figure that out my entire life."

Bubby couldn't stop it. The laughter came unbidden.

"Get in."

Once inside Bubby began to warm to this whole enterprise. The glimpse of Ashley Swanson's legs filled him with longing, but it also kept him in the here and now. Anchored by desire. "Your dad's a nice guy."

Ashley put the keys in the ignition and then looked out the windshield. She didn't comment and her silence put Bubby ill at ease. He was wandering again, out there, looking for his self, for what made him who he was. He wanted to recover that self, reset it, put it back where it belonged. Ashley was a distraction, though, and not a totally unwelcome one. She drove slow at first, south toward one of the bridges. Once in Virginia, she opened it up. "I can see why she went for this one. This baby's got some pep." Bubby held the armrest. This is where it ends. "Tell me," she said. "What's a sweet boy like you doing couped up in your room?"

The sweet boy comment got to him. "I'm taking some time off." He tried to make it seem like he had an important job and had taken leave.

"Busy guy." She smiled, then pressed the accelerator. Bubby's head was thrown back. She shifted gears with authority. Bubby felt safer with her than he did with his mother on that last trip they took together in the Trans Am. "Pressures of life getting to you?"

"You know. With my mom and all." He was outside himself again. Pulling a rope to contain his self-consciousness. Everything about him, his look, his words, weren't his.

She pulled the car off the highway. Out stretching. Bubby

watched her. This is what drove men to fling themselves off bridges, pummel other men, hit the rock, lose their fortune, minds. It was also the source of all hope and promise. He wished Abe could be here to see it. Her eyes. Her chest. Her legs. He was nowhere and he was here. *This is enough*, he thought. If it all fell apart tomorrow, at least he could say he had this.

She leaned in through the window. "Your turn."

"I, uh."

"Come on."

She drove on looking for a large parking lot without cars in it. Bubby needed to impress her. Easing into the lot. Parked and got out. They switched places. *It's just a glorified go cart.* Nothing to crash into. She briefed him on the relationship between the clutch and the gearshift. He got the car moving though, stalled, turned the key, started again. After a few stops and starts he was able to roll it along.

"There you go, Bubby."

The power of it all. The pleasure in satisfying his passenger. It had to be as good as the act, a boy behind the wheel of a sports car trying to impress a girl. Then he looked at her smiling demonically. Stung again. Inside him dying.

Bubby asked Brandy if she wanted to drive his mom's car to the hospital. She quickly rebuffed him, saying, "Come on, Bubby, there are no papers on that car." They got in the clunker, Bubby saying prayers silently to St Dymphna. *It's in your hands, my saint, please help hold her together.* His fingers were knotted. The sounds of her car's engine straining calmed him somewhat. Was his mother completely out there, drifting, still? All the things he feared coming to a ferocious head. What if she just disappears one day? He sat in the feeling. The pain of it all. And then this sliver of hope. She'd pull herself out of it. There's nothing stopping her from getting better. St Dymphna would make it happen, shine your light down on her. *And while you're at it, keep that guy from crashing through the window. I'll help myself. I'll pick myself up. I'll be better, Mom. You'll see.*

The hospital, that blot, rose up ahead, causing him the same drained feeling. It all went south. He lost the saint; couldn't remember all the vows he'd made to himself. Just a lost boy again.

It took Carrie Welter all the energy she had to make sentences and to pretend to be a loving and capable parent. Bubby was used to this dance now, and the ward itself and all its occupants didn't scare him anymore. Not even the woman pulling strands of her hair until they were about to fall out in clumps. The man on the sill, he too was a friend. *These are just people.* Stuck, yes, but not choosing this, striving to make it all right again. Those patients in the movie not being able to choose their fate. Carrie stared. "I quit watching TV."

It seemed to take all of her energy to turn her head to the right and look over at her son. "That's good."

They were strangers on a bus bench. Death was hanging in the air. Bubby was enveloped in it. "Schoolwork is going well, too." There was a little lie in there. "Mr. Swanson's daughter is staying with him."

She said "Oh." Faked chirpiness.

Bubby scratched his nose. "He sends his best."

Carrie ran her hands through her hair. She was still pretty to Bubby. Bags under her eyes, thinner, but still. "Tell him I said hi." No emotion in her voice. She looked away from him. Bubby felt this great distance even though they were sitting not two feet apart. He was on an iceberg, alone, floating on a frigid sea. It might be that way for some time.

"When are you getting out of here?"

"Bub." She cried into a tissue.

Mom, perk up. Come on. You can if you just push a little harder. He looked down. "Oh."

"Bubby. I'm no g…" The weeping intensified.

Bubby put his hand out and she took it. Some power filled him. He was no longer the boy who had peed himself, or ever shrank from a challenge. Now, he was the young man who could climb the ropes in gym, the one who could approach the girl, get his work done, hold his head up high, walk Stone until he developed blisters, drop weight, live an honest and respectable life.

She cried harder.

"You'll be ok, Mom. I know it." He looked over at the hair puller. She was taking a break from it and was hurriedly flipping through the pages of a newspaper.

"Oh, Bub," she said. "My Bub."

Ashley was watching TV and chain-smoking in Tony's living room, and he was in the den putting words to pictures, or at least attempting to. There had to be space between them. He was getting more and more irked by her presence every day. She sponged money, ate on his dime, and made no attempt to better her life or share with him how she might do that. He was dumbfounded. Looking in her eyes he couldn't find any signs of life. A vacuum. After berating himself for a few minutes for his frustration, he started once again to settle on the predicament he found himself in. He was the one that reached out. And now she was here, and he was getting nothing out of her. Just bits and pieces about her relationship out west, how it turned ugly. There were gaps in the stories, and Tony was filling them up with horrid imaginings. She had turned to criminality. These thoughts burned a hole in his chest. There was something vacant about her. She didn't understand her story. Only indulging her base needs. *But, more than that*, he thought. *She was plotting and scheming.* He tried to stop these thoughts when they came. There it was though. *What is she capable of?* He brought her here with his letters and now he regretted it. Dug a hole for himself. Kick her out. Confront her. You've got to come up with some sort of plan, Ashley. You're adrift. Not a kid anymore and I can't help you, nor am I responsible any longer for raising you. He buried his face in his hands and sighed.

The TV went silent. Ashley was in the doorway. *Do it now*, he thought. He looked out at Que. A streetlamp was flickering. He took her in. "Going out for a beer," she said. He held this person when she was a baby, sure he never dropped her, accompanied her to her first day of school, kissed her on her graduation and now he didn't know her, had no idea what ran around and through her mind. "Can I get a twenty?"

"Ashley. I can't keep doing this. You've got to come up with a plan."

She only stared at him with a dark expression. It scared him.

"We need to talk."

Again, the blank stare. What? It said. You don't love me anymore. Can't even look after your only child? "Can't we do it tomorrow?" The little girl, reaching, leaning in, imploring, using what she had, what she knew she could employ. How kids go from exalting their parents to depreciating them, swinging back and forth. Tony only saw the demeaning side.

Pull her close, he thought, the urge came on so strong. Let her go, the harder one to deal with. See if she can handle "no." Push her out the door. A pendulum swinging within him. He reached into his pocket and passed her the twenty. She snatched it out of his hand. It felt cruddy. "This is it."

The blank stare embedded with a phantom glaze. "I'll have something by tomorrow." Tony said, *yeah right*, in his mind. And then she was gone. Five minutes later the door to the apartment was opening. Out she went. Tony hardened. He got up and paced. Then he went to the window and watched his little girl walk into the night, into the danger, into the great world. And guilt and sorrow were about to devour him. There she is, then turning right, then out of view. Tony let the desperation overcome him. It was like a flu coming on.

Chapter 10

Ashley got him talking. She knew how to use every resource she had. She and Bubby were sipping sodas at Scott's. Ashley would smile seductively nearly every time Bubby uttered a word, even if it was just an "um, well, you know." She thought about the Trans Am, she thought about money and where they had obtained it, she had greed shining in her eyes, and knew she was keeping it well-disguised.

"You have nice eyes," she said. "You look like you're eighteen."

Bubby looked out the window. He wanted Abe to pass by. Let him become embroiled in jealousy. Or better yet, Redson. "Thanks."

"Where'd you get to be so cute and sweet?"

This was too much. He got caught looking at her cleavage. Ashley ran a hand through her hair. He had no idea how to answer. Not once had he been asked a question like that.

"Your mom is doing better, I hear."

"Yeah. She'll be back on her feet soon."

"Where's she from?" Ashley took a sip of her drink.

"Upstate New York."

"What did her parents do?"

The inside of Bubby's head began to tickle. "Her father owned a company." It was difficult, but Bubby managed to keep eye contact with her. "He made investments, too. He died last year."

Ashley sat up straighter and did that thing with hands and hair again.

"What kind of investments?"

"I don't know. But they were good ones."

"Oh?"

"It was quite a windfall."

She took a sip of her drink and looked about the place. "Hence the car."

"Yeah."

"Well," she said. "Money isn't everything."

"Right!"

Bubby looked at her chest for a beat too long and she noticed it. "What say we go for a walk in that park over there?"

They were outside the church in their ring smoking and talking and Bubby was thinking about Saint Dymphna. She'd remedy all of them, me too, Mom as well. This unknown woman bathing the pain of the mentally ill. She lived on, somehow still caring for all of them. Bubby wanted to open a space for himself in the circle, start divulging his inner life in front of all these other souls who would hang on his words, take him in as one of their own. Was it too early to become an alcoholic?

"I know that scene," Ashley said.

Bubby didn't comprehend.

"Solve your own problems, I say. Don't go around advertising them."

Bubby had a line of sentences ready, and all of them began with 'but'. They walked across the softball diamond and sat on the seesaw. Ashley flung him up in the air and his desire transformed, went from intense to soft, almost so that he couldn't locate it anymore. The sky was flashing sunset colors and he saw a pinprick of orange off in the direction of the western sky. It grew in size and ferocity, and it was coming their way. Ten different kinds of gases contained in the ball, and the heat they gave off, were about to suck them up into the fireball's innards. Bubby ducked. As if that might save him.

"You're so handsome and smart, you know that?"

Bubby looked down. His mind couldn't catch up with his body's raging messages. And just like that, the lust returned, nearly lifted him, and knocked him off his feet.

"I'll bet your mother bought you some nice things with some of your inheritance."

Bubby looked west. The fireball had swerved slightly and was no doubt crossing the Camotop now. He pictured it plunging into the water, extinguished. He got off the seesaw and swiveled his head, looking in all directions. He had a painful urge to get in sweatpants and lie in front of the TV, the remote plastered to his chubby fingers. Brandy could be there in the apartment, but not too close, and she had to remain quiet.

"She bought the car. And I got some suits and clothes. We were looking for houses out in the suburbs, before, well…"

Ashley got up. "You'll have to try them on for me." She was a cub reporter.

"It's only money."

Ashley did the hair twirl. "You're so right! You know that. You're a smart kid."

"Money does make the world go round, though."

Ashley came up to within a foot of his face. "Yes! It makes the world go round." She put a finger out and tapped at his nose. He couldn't bring it down, and it would stay like that, the feel of finger on nose until he got inside his apartment and met Brandy.

Once inside, Bubby gave in. Brandy was doing a crossword at

the kitchen table, she enquired about his whereabouts. Bubby said he was at Abe's. The remote felt foreign in his hand. Thoughts of Ashley, her nearness, brought it up again, so he began thinking of Bromberg and the grey chest hairs poking out of his shirt. The chalk scratching across the black. Plotting Odysseus' journey home. Icarus' flight, wax melting. Waiting for that bell to release them all. Hormones lined up, released by the clang.

    He remembered what shows were on on a Friday night. He scoured the channels, which didn't take long. He wanted that Love Boat to sink. That would be a show. TV. Old habits die hard. He clicked off the set and stared out in front of him. She was in his bloodstream, sneaking through him. The glory and stealth and danger of Ashley Swanson. It came up again. He put a pillow over it in case Brandy appeared. When it was safe, he got up and went to the window and stared out at the Trans Am. *Now that I can drive it*, he thought, *why not get down there and take her for a spin*. Reason beat out impulsivity. Giving up that thought, he went into his room and took care of the task at hand, her cleavage, and her scent, all of her, alive in his imagination. Afterwards, he did twenty pushups and fifty sit ups, then planned his walk for the following day. A sudden urge to ask Tony to accompany him lurched up in his thoughts.

The club was called 1st Amendment, and on this night was filled with young professionals. Ashley scoped out the place and finally settled on her prey. He was wearing a starched blue shirt, the bottom of which was now slipping out of the waistband of his pants. Had that macho, hungry look. Enough in his pockets to pay for it. Clean cut and wasted. The lights came up at two. She positioned herself outside, leaning against the rail that skirted the stairs leading into the place. She was drunk enough not to care, sober enough to be in control. Here he came, ringed by his cohorts. She was wearing tight jeans and a shirt with frills. Once he came out, she threw that mischievous, wanting grin in his direction. He had nothing else to do but talk to her.

"Waiting for me?" He was trying to hide the slur in his voice.

"You bet," Ashley said.

A gaggle of people came out. The guy, whose name turned out to be Trevor, waved them all away. A female friend of his looked from him to Ashley, then scowled at Trevor. The rest of them streamed out into the street.

Ashley looked right into his eyes. She portioned out the manner in which she released her charms, but none of them were lost on Trevor. They walked around the block. Ashley pulled a flask from her purse and handed it to Trevor who, when he passed it back, watched what he thought was Ashley taking a large gulp, when in reality she didn't swallow any of the liquor.

"Where did you come from?" As if she weren't standing in front of him.

"You're the second person that's asked me that today." She pulled out a cigarette and Trevor lit it with a slight shake in his hand. "In that exact formulation."

"Well?"

"Listen Trevor," she pulled out a semi-gnarled joint and lit it. She was careful to take small tokes while Trevor hit it hard. "How 'bout we continue this private party at your place?"

He took another large puff off the joint. "Sure, I'm just up the road."

Ashley surveyed the living room while Trevor peed. It was clean, had nice furniture and spelled out, if not a ton of it, but money.

Trevor came right up to her and put his hands on her waist, tugged her close. They kissed and he pawed at her. He gave her a small shove and she was on the couch. Nearly smothering her now. She tried to find the air to breathe. With a heave she got him off of her. "How much do you think is a good price?"

"What?"

"This is a private party."

"What? We're negotiating now?"

It was at this point, as it was in all of these encounters, that Ashley would become afraid. Not a rush of fear, but the shape of it forming in her chest. Was he a cop? Too smart? Too upstanding? Violent? It was the last one that scared her the most. "Two hundred for an hour."

"You little…"

"Everything has a price. Am I wrong? And this will be worth your while. Trust me."

"I knew this was too good…"

He got up and found the money in a drawer, the rest in his wallet. She could have a small field day in here. They kissed and smoked on the sofa. Then he got on her. He had smoked and drunk too much and now sat there conked out. Luckily, Ashley had collected the money before any of this happened. She had slipped the bills neatly in her purse and began to untangle herself from Trevor's clutch, snapped in front of his face. The weed worked well. The clap in front of his face this time, then she did a survey of the one bedroom she found herself in. She went into his top drawer in the closet, pocketed cufflinks, a watch, and a silver ring. A smile flashed on her face. She already knew the location of the pawn shop she'd visit the next day. She collected herself in the mirror and prepared to leave. One last look at the passed-out form of Trevor on the couch. Pleasure doing business with you, ran through her head. She was sure she closed the door as quietly as possible upon her departure.

Chapter 11

Bubby was in the driver's seat of the parked Trans Am playacting. The music poured out of the speakers, he had it up loud. *Well, if she wants to see me, you can tell her I'm easily found.* He shut her down and got out of the car, stepping into reality. He looked up at his place and for a moment spotted his mother pacing the living room, waving a cigarette in the air, plotting, devising, losing it. Head on fire. Arms akimbo. He loved and missed her still.

Scott in his element wiping down the counter. Abe came in wearing a white T shirt and shorts. Must have been the Taekwondo, or some other earthly force, that kept Bubby's friend on that even keel. Scott questioned them lightly, then returned with two chocolate milks. "We'll always be kids to them," Abe said. "Even when we're thirty." Abe ordered half the left side of the menu. Bubby went with a Western Omelet. "What's to tell, Bub?"

"Ashley Swanson."

Abe waved his hand in the air.

"How's everything at Carter?" Bubby took a sip of his drink. The sugar carried voltage.

"What's to tell?"

"No intrigues?"

The food came. Scott smiled. Abe attacked it. "Nah."

"Listen, Abe. I want to take the car out. Brandy will be gone tomorrow."

Abe went bug eyed. "Are you out of your mind?"

"Ashley will be with me."

Abe stopped chewing. "This is the time to be cautious."

"I'll just take her around the block."

"Who is this Ashley and why does she want to be hanging around a fifteen-year-old for? That's what I want to know."

Bubby felt like he'd slipped on a rock down at Stone. "She likes me."

"She likes you, huh?"

"Abe, come on."

"As your lawyer, I advise against it."

Bubby went up the stairs in twos. He had more energy than he'd had in a long time. Swanson was out picking up his paper. "Hey Tony."

"Bub. Looking good."

"What's in the paper?"

Tony scanned the front page. Bubby saw the story about the shooting, top of the page. He read the words "young student shot down after leaving bar". Detectives and the press mobilized. Bubby wondered if it was Lindsay.

Tony put the paper under his arm. "It's a nice day."

He peeked past Swanson to try and get a look at his siren. She was out cold on the couch.

"Are you doing your urban hiking today?"

"Yeah."

"Would you like some company? I won't bring the camera."

Bubby scratched his nose. "Sure." Swanson looked at him.

"If it's an imposition…"

"No. We could do that."

"Let me just change." Bubby peeked in at Ashley who was still lying dead on the sofa. She hadn't adjusted her position.

He had hidden the car keys in his sock drawer. He spun them around his fingers and fell into a daydream. Racing down the road with Ashley at his side. She'd start undressing and then...

Brandy stared. "Bubby! Mr. Swanson is waiting. Get yourself together."

Out the door the two of them went. The scents of renewal, a tingle in his nose. A silky layer of hope covered his malaise. Swanson was experiencing the moment of regrowth for the first time. His head sprang out in front of him. Bubby thought that this was the time for a lecture, but it didn't come. They walked down the trail that led to Stone accompanied by a warm breeze. The creek was dead. They hopped over a few stones and made their way to solid ground. Swanson stopped and halted Bubby with his arm. He looked up in a tree and pointed out a few birds and then named them. Although Bubby heard their whistle, he couldn't pick them out in their forest perch.

They walked under the bridge. Bubby was glad they didn't go up to the street. Standing on the bridge would have given him too many options. Swanson was spry for an older man. At times, Bubby struggled to keep pace. It felt good to be walking at such a fast clip. The thoughts finally evened out. Bubby felt strong, that he could take on anything now. The sweat collected on his forehead and leaked from his armpits. The forest on either side of Stone grew denser. Bubby wouldn't let anyone hurt him. He did his daily, silent prayer to Dymphna. It went something like this: *My saint, keep my mom healthy and happy. Set her right, and keep me from doing something stupid, something that will drive her further away. Make me a better son.*

They walked on. It got hotter. They sat on a bench and listened to the sounds of bikers whizzing by the asphalt chewing up the rubber on their tires. Bubby opened his mouth to say something. "She's getting better." He spoke in nearly a whisper.

"That's such good news, Bubby."

"Yeah. It's just."

Swanson waited patiently.

"I drove her to it."

"No, you did not. She's ill, Bubby."

"Before, I did some things…"

Swanson put his hand on Bubby's shoulder. "We all do things, sometimes things we're not proud of. Be gentle on yourself, Bubby. Go easy."

As they were walking back toward home a picture of him arose in Bubby's mind. Carrie Welter had erased Felix Welter from hers and Bubby's life once he disappeared and Bubby had never seen a picture of his father. Just then, on the trail, he started to wonder. Does he have long sideburns, a temper, long legs, the voice and ideas of Tony Swanson, the wherewithal to take a long walk with his son; is he alive? A burning desire to see the man filled Bubby, then just as fast as it entered did it disappear. He crept away in the night and in the darkness he'd have to remain. The surroundings slipped away, and Bubby listened to his breath going in and out.

Ashley was dressed in her tight jeans and a shirt that gave a plentiful view of her breasts. It drove him to heights of aggravation. It was past four. Bubby had done his work for the day. Words and ideas were starting to make more sense to him, and the novel was half-read. The TV was still dark, and its charms had gone stale. Brandy was at the market and Ashley had appeared at the Welter's door in the aforementioned outfit. "Hi, Bub." Using the nickname.

Bubby looked in several directions, her face being none of them.

She leaned to the side and pouted her lips. "Taking care of your business?" Before Bubby could say anything, she had moved past him and entered the apartment. Her scent left a trail, and it nearly knocked the boy over. She leaned down and touched the edge of the couch, then picked up a photo of Bubby and his mom. "You're definitely her son." She sat down on the couch and crossed her legs, then shortly after, recrossed them. The shock of the desire floored him. It came on fast, and he was sure he'd break into pieces. "Good looking mom with a stud for a son." Bubby wanted to flee. The lower half of his body began to go numb. "What say you and me go for a ride in the old fire-engine-red whip out there?" Had anyone, ever, said no to this person? She got up and came closer to the boy. His lungs stopped working. She put her hand up and gave him an affectionate pat on the cheek. "I've got something I want to discuss with you, Bub. You'll really want to hear this. Now, where are those keys?"

He was powerless. In the bedroom, sock drawer, keys. They were out the door in a hurry. She drove the speed limit. She wheeled the car around traffic circles. The martyred soldiers winked at them. Bubby watched the scenery go by but saw none of it. Stealing looks at her legs, wondering what she had cooking. Bubby was also imagining a life where he'd never be able to speak to a woman. Destined to live out his life alone, head crammed with thoughts that would never be spoken. Heading east. Bubby ate a nail and made a cuticle. She picked up the pace. He spied her painted toenails that rested on the gas pedal. Alone and forgotten and eventually ending up in a place like the one his mother now resided in.

They turned onto Columbia. She put her hand on the side of

the door and slowed the car down. There were shops and apartment buildings on this part of the street. There was a sign draped across one of the shops that said For Sale. Bubby's face began to itch. He was jumping out of the car and running crazily up and down the street looking for someone to take him in. It was madness. What was she doing with a kid like him?

"This is it, Bub. My place."

"What?"

"The Daily Grind."

"The what…?"

"My coffee shop. I'm buying it. Come on."

They parked and got out of the car. Bubby looked in the window. He had to use his imagination. "Picture it," she said. "Full of people, reading, laughing, gabbing, espresso machines gurgling, gourmet coffee, jazz music. It will liven up this block. People coming together over good coffee. I got a good price too." Ashley smiled and straightened up. The way she held herself spoke to Bubby more than what she said. She talked on about buying instead of renting and who she already had lined up as investors. "Bub. I want you and your mom to get in on this. I've got the business plan all drawn up. I can show it to you, and you can bring it to your mom. Look at this block. It's got growth potential written all over it. Don't just picture it now. See it two, five years down the line. I'm telling you. The place will be all mine. People flooding in and out of the place. Pastries, cakes, cookies, and atmosphere. That's what I'm aiming for – a vibe. Come and get in on it, Bub. You can be an executive, so to speak. Pick books and music. Be involved."

The windfall. It was out there in the open already.

He looked in and saw a board lying horizontal over a

disheveled floor, paper, and other debris. "I'll talk to her about it."

Bubby didn't think about Ashley's business idea, nor did he see her for four days. The night of the viewing he lay in bed with his arms crossed behind his head. He was thinking about his mom. It had been a month now and she was still languishing in the junkyard of madness. His twice weekly visits helped rid him of guilt. But he still felt the shame and the sense of loss. His mind raking over scenarios, ways he could have staved off her illness. He thought about the place she was in. Shoddy, decrepit, lonely, and forlorn. He couldn't stop it from creeping up and then overtaking him. The sobs surprised him. It was pure emotion let loose. Clean release. Brandy heard it from the living room. She came to his door and stood there.

The dome atop the halls of power just down the road had popped off and all the legislators and the contents of the building had turned to liquid fool's gold, and was pouring out and down the streets of Bubby's city. That's what the crying felt like. But now it had halted. His eyes went squishy. The light on the desk shone in his face and he saw shapes in the form of shadows on the wall. A monster with a hatchet. And yes, the face of Ashley Swanson, the outline of her body. Clarity now. He saw her. She flickered into view, then disappeared. He had her in his mind then she was gone again. The true Ashley. What was the true Ashley? The shadow trying to engulf him? Or the girl next door. Bubby swam through the desire and got to something deeper. But that didn't hold for long. He was back to being obsessed with her. Sure that he would do anything to keep her attention on him. A prisoner of his youth.

Bubby finally got around to reading the business plan. Lack of experience kept him from getting a firm understanding of what was written. She had put work into it. He did pick up on a few typos. Ashley was selling the experience, and the plan was light on numbers. At the bottom was a line for a signature and another for the amount to commit to. Jess Bagley money. He was sure his mother would go for, if not fifty, then surely twenty-five. The business plan assured a rapid return on the investment. But what did he know? Part of him saw the whole thing as an avenue leading him toward Ashley Swanson's tits.

Unbeknownst to Bubby – after the viewing and the car ride home, Ashley had pocketed the keys to the Trans Am.

Brandy hadn't been able to get a read on Ashley Swanson. What she did see, though, she didn't much care for. She was driving the jalopy down Canal. Some stain in her eyes. Bubby had his window open and spring scents rushed into the car.

"It looks good, though," Bubby said.

She remained quiet. Her thoughts were elsewhere. Her father. The cause of his death. Her sister who wasn't getting better. Her own life and its responsibilities. The heaviness of a Wednesday afternoon in late April, going to visit a beloved family member who was locked up, nearly all her freedom stripped from her. "It seems thin."

"It's a coffee shop. No more, no less."

"Bubby. At the end of the day, it's none of my business."

He held the plan in his hand. The end of the hall. It got to him once again. She wasn't in there. Brandy gave Carrie a big hug, then retreated to the cafeteria.

"Mom."

"Oh, Bub. Just the man I wanted to see." Her words were trying to emerge from a ball of cotton that was stuck in her throat. She put her hand up and caressed his face. It was Ashley doing it. For a second. He looked in his mother's eyes and still saw the vacancy. One of the assistants suggested a short walk around the grounds. That person accompanied them to the door and waited. The buzzer that would open that door to the outside was ominous sounding. Once there, Carrie Welter stopped. She looked behind her, she stepped forward. Bubby and the assistant waited patiently. The sun had yet to go down and the trees had a lemony, dusk-like color to them. Carrie stopped by a bench and looked around her. She seemed not able to place herself in her surroundings.

"Let's sit down, Mom."

She nodded. They sat and stared off into the distance. The garden was lush. Other patients milled about.

"How are you, Bub?"

He looked into his lap. "I'm okay, Mom."

She patted his thigh but couldn't look at him. He wanted to tell her things to try and cheer her up, but he couldn't bring himself to say anything positive, in fact, anything at all. He held Ashley's business plan, sure now of what he would do.

"I miss you," he said.

Another pat. "Oh Bub." He wondered what they had her on. Strong stuff no doubt, he told himself. A flash. His pilfering some of her tablets. Guilt fell on him, and he nearly told her of his transgression. "Listen, sweety." She finally looked over at him, briefly. Then she stared out into the depths of the garden. "Let me tell you something. Your grandfather. I never told you this. He took his own…"

Bubby leaned forward. Path, way, company public?

"Now, no one should do it. No one, and promise me... but the genes, Bub." Her voice trailed off, leaving Bubby perplexed.

It wasn't until he got back home and was lying in bed with his hands behind his head that it hit him. An internal itch rushed him out of bed. He paced his room, not sure where to put all the energy. The living room provided no shelter. He stared at the shut off TV and saw his reflection. The phone sat there beckoning to him, but he didn't know of anyone he could call. He could try the ward, maybe get his mom. It was after midnight, though. Brandy would talk him down if he went to her. Back in his room, he hit the floor and did two sets of sit ups and two of pushups. The rush of endorphins settled his mind somewhat, yet his thoughts were still pinned on his grandfather and how he took his exit. The one-way ride administered by his own will. He picked up the novel and read for a half an hour. He was getting the feel for the writing style and the characters were coming alive. And then irritating thoughts. His mother lying on the floor that day, the bottle of pills emptied out. The rush to get to the phone.

Was that the moment when the boy's childhood had begun to come to an end?

Bubby walked all the way to the central public library the next day and did his schoolwork in a corral in a quiet corner. Stronger than an ox now. All the flab was gone. Brandy cooked wholesome foods that increased the boy's strength. It gave his mind a kick too. The words he read made more sense. The math problems weren't as daunting. He'd be back in school that next Monday, which he was actually looking forward to. Still the sticky thoughts clung to his mind. At times he felt he could sidestep them or let them glide through his brain without digging into them. Others, he felt them nudging him, making him restless. He couldn't help but thinking about his future. *Seize on one thing, Bub.* He was sure he'd graduate in two years. The grades will go up. There were those comforts. What about the greater future? It was murky. Every time he tried to settle on an objective, one thing, it all vanished: job, wife, kids, house, death. Forever loading the dishwasher and unclogging the sink. What of his mother's fate? He saw her on that ledge, burned out, at wits end, struggling and never finding her footing again. Bubby would have to pick her up from the floor, Mother in the fetal position, a bottle of pills next to her. Craving safety and protection knowing no one can really protect anyone else. She would have to do that herself.

Abe and Bubby sat at Scott's in the corner. They had sodas and fries on the table in front of them.

"Back Monday," Bub said.

"How does it feel?"

"Good actually. I'm too much on my own. Not sure this furlough was the right thing."

"I could see that," Abe said. "It'll be good to have you back."

"And all the bs.?"

"Don't fall for it, I guess."

Bubby looked down. "There's so much of it."

"You're standing straighter now. This Ashley chick?"

Bubby was still looking down. He felt his chest go prickly. "Mom."

Abe looked at his friend with sympathetic eyes.

"She'll get out," Bubby said. "And then what?"

"Those kinds of hospitals are better than they were twenty

years ago."

"It's fucked up."

Abe put his drink down. Tony Swanson came in the place and sat at the counter. Abe and Bubby watched him order a beer. He looked over in the boys' direction, came over. "Fellas!"

"Hey, Tony."

"Fries good today?"

Abe said, "Scott's got it down."

"I'll leave you two to it." Swanson looked at Bubby and then put his hand on his shoulder. Bubby watched him drink up and leave the place, no doubt off to some show.

"He's cool."

"I know," Bubby said. Abe held a fry up to his face then began to nibble on it. He watched his friend freeze. Abe turned around and watched her sashay into the place. She waved at Bubby and ordered a beer. Scott looked her over trying to ascertain her age, then gave her a bottle of beer and a glass. Outside the light had gone. Ashely came over. Bubby was about to get up and leave. Make some excuse and wiggle out of there.

"Boys."

Abe studied her as she looked into Bubby's eyes. Abe couldn't make sense of her. After the lust had been cooled by his thought processes, he began analyzing again from a place of calm objectivity. At first, he was scared, then sizing her up, he got angry. He saw no good coming from this person. His friend should have nothing to do with her. Ashley put her hand on Bubby's cheek which sent shockwaves through the boy. "You two enjoy yourselves. Don't stay out too late." Bubby's face cracked. He couldn't help it. He found himself turning around to take in the view.

"That's Ashley," Bubby said.

"I figured that," Abe said.

"She's on fire."

"Yeah well, you know it's not an option."

"Don't burst my bubble."

"There's something in her."

Bubby cocked his head. "There's something in all of us."

"I know. Never mind."

Bubby talked to Brandy that night. They were sitting in the living room. Brandy was watching a rerun of a cop show that Bubby had seen. She was knitting a pair of booties for her niece. Bubby watched her fingers work. *It was the path to enlightenment*, he thought. You didn't have to wear a robe and sit under a tree on a mountaintop to achieve it. One could get it by immersing oneself in any kind of task, and that's what he wanted to find. The path to a higher way of being. Yet, across the hall sat a vixen, a person that he was about to give a large sum of money to.

He went into his mother's drawer in the bedroom and took out her check book. He found a document lying there with Carrie Welter's signature on it and practiced writing it on a sheet of paper. He wondered, briefly and carelessly, if this wasn't the price he was paying to see those breasts of Ashley's, to get his hands on them. A shove in his mind. Sense, then irrationality, all governed by his youthful lust, which had no beginning and no end. About to fall through a crack in the floor, he put the check book in his pocket. It was hard to know what he was thinking just then if anything at all. He was on the verge of something. At the edge of a cliff where underneath lay a chasm, and in that massive crevice stood the body of Ashley Swanson.

He waited for Brandy to go to bed, twiddling his thumbs on the couch. He pressed it down. It had a life of its own, twisting and writhing. He did fifty pushups on the living room floor. First it got in the way. It kept hitting the floor before his chest did. He turned and did fifty crunches. It went down. Afterwards, he wasn't sure where he was. The real Bubby Welter had left his body. He was a husk. But do this he must.

He went over. She answered the door with a glow. Ashley had on a sweatshirt and a pair of jeans. Bubby tried to remember what it meant to be able to speak. She ushered him into the place. Tony was still out. "Bubby. You're a sight for sore eyes." She led him to the couch. He sat and watched her get a folder. She came back and began laying papers on the coffee table. All the things written on them swam lost through Bubby's mind. Then she reached down and took off her pullover. Bubby was greeted with the sight of those breasts, the ones he'd spent hours imagining, their texture, the squishiness, allure, all of it. He'd done a number over them in the confines of his own room. "It's all coming together. I got two people to come in yesterday." She threw her hair back with a jerk. "Imagine, me, a small business owner. It's all so surreal. But I knew I had it in me."

Run.

She leaned over. He could smell the scent of lust and feel the agony. She kissed him on the cheek, then turned his head with a finger and kissed him again, this time on the lips. Electrical currents ran through him. She took his hand and brought it to her chest. "Caress them, Bubby." His hand landed on her right breast, but it didn't move. Planted there. "Move it around." He did as she told. It topped anything he'd done up to this point. "Rub them. That's it." He moved his hands around on them. The ceiling didn't fall so he kept going. "Kiss them." He did that too. She arched her back.

Moments flew by. He lost some of his inhibitions. He

continued to rub and kiss. After a few minutes Ashley got up and released Bubby from his activities. "You're so sweet and so cute."

"This is going to be big." She saw the checkbook peeking out of his pocket. "Get in Bubby. You and your mom, you won't regret it."

He took out the check book. If that meant more rubbing and caressing. Sense hadn't completely returned to him, but he managed to write out a check for $50,000 and hand it over to Ashley. Was his hand shaking?

"Oh, Bubby. I'll get your papers to you in a few days. "This is monumental. It's a journey."

Yes, but can I rub your tits some more?

She put the pullover back on. Bubby stood there waiting. A minute later she was showing him to the door. When he got back home, he went into his room and let fly. Then he went to the living room window and stared down at the red car. His mind was on a highway. Urges calmed but still settled on those breasts. Sleep came like a drug.

He was asking his mom about him again. His father had been on his mind for some time now. Carrie looked off into the distance, at the trees and flowers, then back at the building of her confinement. She had to have the conversation. It had been a while since she had broached it with her son. "Felix Welter. What can I say? He was a restless soul. I always thought he had his heart in the right place, Bub. But if someone could avoid getting into trouble, then it wasn't your father. From one bad business idea to another. Factor in the…" She seemed to grow tired. Bubby looked at her then away. Her eyes were trained on everything in the garden and at nothing at all. Bubby felt like she might slump over. He readied himself to catch her if she tumbled off the bench. He had to let it go for now.

She found a local bank to cash the check. Walked out into broad daylight with a bag full of cash. She was whistling. That night she dug the car keys out of a pocket in her bag and made her way down to the street. Ashley looked left and right, then started whistling again. The Trans Am made that sweet humming roar of a sound when she started it. She took one last look up at the apartment building, thought of the open road and then maneuvered the car onto Que. She turned the radio on and found her way north. She belted out the lyrics and began pushing harder on the accelerator. West now. The window cracked. Warm air soothing, nothing on her mind, just west – go in that direction. Faster now. On the highway, dodging in and out of traffic. In the oncoming lane, just to test herself. A semi approached. Close, closer, right at her. At the last minute she swerved back to her lane, to safety. For now. Try it again. A van coming on. She played chicken. Close now. She swerved back.

Forty hours later she had reached the coast. Car parked. Waves relentless. It was night. She took off all her clothes and jumped into the surf. The moonlight poured down. The water was cold. She dunked her head in and said something to herself, but it didn't come out in a clear fashion. Up on the surface, a red glow to the horizon. Out there. China and India and other exotic places. When she got in the car she felt for the bag under the seat. It was still there. Under the light of the moon, she made her way n orth, stopped at a motel, peeled off some bills, got to her room and slept for the next fifteen hours. She didn't dream of anything at all. And if she had, all of the dreams had flown off into the ether upon her waking.

Chapter 12

Bubby sat with Brandy at the kitchen table. He could feel in his gut that something was wrong. The sun wasn't sure it was doing what it was supposed to be doing and the light in the apartment felt artificial. He slurped at his granola and when Brandy got up to use the bathroom, he walked over to the living room window and peered out. It was just as he had feared but it still gave him a start. The car was gone. When he got back down from the mental heights he had climbed, hands held in prayer, the car was still nowhere to be seen. He braved the short walk over to Swanson's. He didn't know anything about any small business venture. In fact, Ashley and her stuff were gone when he woke up. A quick feel and vision of those breasts flashed in Bubby's mind.

"I gave her something," he said.

"What? What did you give her? Please tell me it wasn't money." Tony paced the living room. Bubby could feel the heat coming off the man.

"It was for the business." Bubby was hoarse.

No words from Swanson for a few minutes. Then he pounded his fist in his hand. "I can't believe this. She took it from you, didn't she?"

"She said it was legit. That Mom and I would be partners."

Swanson wanted to shake the kid. "Well, she's gone now."

"She'll come back."

Tony looked out the window. "Lies and deceit. She took us both for a... Don't you see that? She's not coming back. How could you be..." He stopped himself.

Bubby spent the day in his room going over it in his head. The breasts made him do it. *And I'm left here.* With nothing. He consoled himself with the thought that from what his mother had inherited, this didn't make a dent. He wished Ashley and those breasts a pleasant ride to the destination of her choice. Let her bake in it. Have the cops pull her over and find out she was driving an unregistered car, or worse. It was out of his hands now. *She'll get hers,* he thought. It's written somewhere. There's a saying for it. Karma, that's it. Just like the song, *Instant. But are Tony and I ruined?* The ceiling dropped on his foolishness. He couldn't shake the notion that he had been had. Still, he smiled upwards: at least the kiss, the touching, the exhilaration of her body and her caresses. Even if everything was twisted, he had that. The telephone pole would appear in front of her windshield, or maybe it wouldn't, perhaps she would skate into a blissful future, untouched and moving in her blonde bubble, not giving any thought of the mischief she'd caused or the hurt she laid on others. Spared from Karma's deal.

Who knew?

He wasn't breathing any of this to anyone. No one. *Wait*, he thought. *I already told Tony.* It'd have to be between the two of them, and if there was a stain on their relationship, well, Bubby would have to accept that.

The car had been gone for five days. Bubby checked every day. He would squeeze into the ring outside the church and unburden his soul. Unleash all the guilt and shame with compassionate souls. And, surely Abe would understand, he would have done the same thing under sexual pressure. This was the day, though, that his mother was to be let out of the hospital. Brandy made sure the house was extra stocked with food and that it had been scrubbed and cleaned – Bubby even did the bathroom—and was sure to put on some of his nicer clothes. They ate breakfast. Bubby was more talkative than usual. Brandy let him go on. The sky outside was overcast, and the scent of rain came through the windows, maybe even a thunderstorm. Bubby was to turn sixteen in a week. School let out shortly thereafter. Abe told Bubby that his birthday present to him would be a can of whooping, you know, to knock some sense into you.

They were throwing a baseball back and forth on the softball diamond. Both boys had some zip on their throws. The soothing thwack and punch of ball hitting leather, the open sky, kids hopping and sliding on the playground. It took Bubby a lot of effort not to spill it all out to his friend. Honesty and release battling shame and guilt. *Wait! I've been right here before!* The boys increased the distance between them. The throws were still crisp and on the money. Afterwards, they went to the deli and bought energy drinks. They took them outside and slurped up the sugary liquid. *Do it*, Bubby told himself, *I dare you*. Abe commented on the attributes of a girl who was walking by. Bubby looked up into the sun. How long will it shine? At what point will it burn out? He was sure it would be tomorrow or early next week. He didn't know how to pray for help in the situation he found himself in.

"She's coming home this afternoon."

Abe looked into his drink. "That's good."

"What's in store?"

Abe looked at his friend and then out into the space in front of him. "Got me, Bub. But go easy on her."

"What kind of son have I been?"

"I've told you this before." Was Abe agitated? "Go easy on yourself. Too."

Bubby hung his head. "Yeah, you're right."

The church bells began to ring. *Ashley Swanson let me feel her up and I paid a monstrous price for it.*

"I'm going to work at Scott's this summer."

"Good, Abe. I'm going to start looking for a job, too."

They tossed the ball back and forth on the way to Abe's and then parted. Bubby lay in bed. He couldn't picture his mother's face in his mind. He saw her eyes but then that vision departed. Her walk, then nothing. This aggravated him. The skin under her neck, then the motions her arms made when called into action. Her beauty and grace breaking the nervousness. He pictured that red car stopped by the police, Ashley trying to seduce the police officer. Then it crushed and mangled, Ashley crawling from the wreckage. The ceiling was the portal to heaven. Its celestial contents were about to pour down on him. A ladder would drop down and up he'd go. *Oh, how I won't be picked,* he thought. Devon Redson, Kathy Mosely. *I've got to be more.* The humiliation. The being used. The plain idiocy.

Bubby got up and laced up his sneakers. He walked at a good clip to Swain's Point and back. Brandy was putting her things in her purse. "You're going to be all right, Bubby. And your mom will be too. Just find it in your heart to have patience."

He looked in her eyes. "I will. And aunt Brandy. Thank you." They embraced.

From tomorrow it would just be the two of them.

It must have been like coming out of prison.

Carrie Welter was quiet on the way home. Brandy would drive them home, and then decamp for upstate New York. After they had left the parking lot of the hospital, Carrie took one last look back over her shoulder. Her mind was trying to rearrange the facts. She knew it wasn't about being fixed; she was on the ever-stretching highway of repairing. In a soft voice she said, "Bubby, I forgot to tell you how good you look."

"Thanks, Mom."

Then she stared out the windshield. She had been gone for six weeks and now it felt like an eternity. "I've got to get rid of that car."

Bubby shivered.

"It was stolen."

"All for the better." Her voice was still strained.

"Mom, I...uh...I'm glad you're coming home."

Bubby and Carrie walked Brandy down to the jalopy. They hugged and kissed and then she muscled her way into the car and drove off, waving out of the window. Bubby and his mother waved back.

Bubby did the shopping and cleaning while his mother cooked the meals. She was sluggish and often fell into despair, saying things in a downtrodden way. When Bubby spoke, she could be unresponsive. Carrie would sit on the couch and stare at the TV. Bubby was sure she wasn't taking in any of the information being offered up. She rose. "It's your birthday tomorrow, Bub! We must celebrate. Get Abe over here." Then, after saying this she fell back into the mud pit of herself. Bubby wanted to pull the life out of her, get her up, recharge her.

He had to do it. Tony answered the door. He stared at Bubby for a click, then let him into the apartment. The sunlight poured into the room. It spoke of warning.

"I had to come by."

Tony took a deep breath and then smiled weakly, put a hand on Bubby's shoulder. With this touch, Bubby knew that all was forgiven. Tony was mostly sad on account of what his daughter had duped Bubby into doing. Aggravated at his failure as a father. They talked. Bubby said he had started the book that Tony had given him and that he was enjoying it.

"It's going to be a good summer, Bub."

"Yeah." Tony gave him a firm handshake and ushered him toward the door.

And Bubby went back home. Standing outside his door he thought, *this birthday will be for her, not for me.*

Then he opened the door to his apartment, peered around, took in his mother sitting at the dining room table. Everything had changed, it was just the same as it was.

Part 3 − Searching

Chapter 13

Two years rocketed by. He'd grown two and a half inches in that time, and all the flab was gone. It was the end of June. He'd successfully graduated from high school. His Pre-Calculus teacher, Jeff Morton, mercifully gave Bubby a D instead of failing him, allowing the boy to graduate. He'd matriculate at UM College Park in the Fall. Duty. Closeness. Looking out for her.

Carrie woke and rose to a sitting position in her bed. She said the mantras she'd learned: I am worthy, I am strong, I am a unique soul. She went outside and took a short walk. The sunlight was oppressive. It made her want to shield her eyes, her soul, her whole being. She was still volunteering at a place called the Springs. Giving some semblance of hope to people who were down on their heels and their luck. Her body disputed her mind's intentions often. She was moving, though, forward.

Bubby got up and stood in front of the mirror in his boxers. He said it, for it was the truth. "I am Brandon Welter." Stared into his eyes. "That's right. Bubby and all that he was is gone. Brandon. Welter." Abe loved it, said it meant he was going back to his origins, to the true name. His mother said it was a shelving of his youth. Brandon slid into some shorts and went to the dresser where the folder sat. He opened it and found three pictures in there and one slip of paper with an address written on it. In two of the pictures, his father seemed ready, so full of hope.

The third betrayed some inner conflict. The address was the last one his mother had for him.

"I'm okay with your doing this," she had said. "Just try to dial down your expectations."

"Done."

Brandon Welter strapped on his shoes and went out.

He *ran* now.

When he got back, he went down to the car and inspected it. Carrie had bought it for him, second hand, capable, reliable, boring. Blue with a red top. Only 10,000 miles on it. Economical. Nothing like the last one. The address he had was in Fort Collins, Colorado, but, as Carrie had told him, that was a good thirteen, fourteen years before.

"It's a place to start."

In the shower. More of me. He repeated this over and over. Then this one. A fool no more.

The day after, he packed a duffel bag and slung it over his shoulder. "I'll call you from the road." His mother had given him money for the quest. It was enough to get him there, not too much for him to run amok.

Carrie couldn't hold back the tears. "If you find him, tell the guy I said hi."

Brandon laughed. Then he searched his mother's eyes and face, her gestures. A pang, then a relieving kiss on the cheek. She stood there until he had pulled out of the parking space. He could see her waving, so he put his hand out the window and did the same.

Chapter 14

West, then North for a spell, into Pennsylvania. Time to think. Wondering how he and his father had interacted, all the memories elusive. No evidence through photographs. He was just too young. Brandon had created many stories in his head over the years. None of them could be corroborated. Carrie said he wasn't equipped for the job of being a father. Couldn't keep still. Not able to keep from chasing. This all went down back East. They were living in Silver Spring and baby and that life became a prison for him. She gave him this: he worked hard at supporting mother and baby at a variety of jobs. He left a note and then fled. Carrie remembered thinking, "Well, I can't say I didn't see that one coming."

Music helped on the trip west, but there was a lot of time to think. How far and how easily he had been led. Ashley Swanson; a pock mark. He passed a derelict factory, and something leapt up in him. This vast land. I'm in it, enveloped, taken in.

He stopped at a motel and rented a room. Sneakers on. He ran down a cracked sidewalk, felt his heart thumping, aiding him, his friend. Thoughts eventually cooling down to zero, or at least they had become more comfortable to deal with. Highway thrumming to his left. Passed a truck stop and saw all the behemoths crammed into the parking lot. He thought about the ring of people outside the church back home. *No one, I mean no one, can make it out here all alone,* he thought. That's what the poem said. He thought about his mother. After he'd showered, he called her. She was in a good mood which pleased Brandon. New name, new quest, she said. I'm your biggest fan. The new meds in the cabinet, a leveling out. She was committed to the therapy sessions she was attending.

A sliver of Ohio. Pulling off into a rest stop. Asleep right there. Corridors in his mind. Doors flung open, faces peering out. Some familiar, most alien and meant to bring harm to the dreamer. A man with his back to him, speaking, uttering nonsense. Was it a warning? A girl from elementary school with pigtails: Don't do it Bubby. Bubby, no. An open field crammed with flowers, running through them, not caring who or what was on the other side. The monuments. Horses coming to life, braying, soldiers winking at him, all dead, their deeds done. A man sweeping up debris from the pavement where those soldiers perched on the mounts. The end of the hallway at the hospital, then waking with a gasp.

He took an alternate route through Indiana. A hitchhiker appeared. Why not? It was a woman who looked to be in her early twenties, if not younger. Brandon slowed. *If she murdered me, she murdered me.* She ran to the car, opened the door, and threw her bag in the back. Seemingly unafraid that *he* would murder *her*. "You're a lifesaver. Willamina."

They shook hands. "Brandon Welter. How far are you going?"

"Des Moines. You?"

"Colorado."

She had a big, open face with bulging, alluring brown eyes. Her tanned legs rested easily beneath her. Her smell wouldn't be considered pleasant, but the odor she gave off of sweat gave Brandon a rise. Life lived. Scents accompanying that living. She wanted to hear about him, so he talked, tentative at first, sparing all the messiness. It had been some days since he'd spoken to anyone, so the words felt strange leaving his mouth. She asked such pertinent questions in a giving fashion. She was grateful for the lift.

He told her about his mission.

"And when you find him?"

He took a long time to answer. "Just to see him and talk to him."

"High hopes?"

"Maybe."

"Who knows maybe you'll be pleasantly surprised." Willamina talked about her family, her exploits, her life. She was at ease speaking. She was applying to law school, had a sister who was recovering from a drug problem, and believed that there was a piece of something good in even the lowest cretin. Brandon raised his eyebrows.

They got a motel on the border of Illinois and Iowa. Willamina led him there. She had no restraint. He was grateful. It happened fast and ferocious. Brandon married his good luck. Becoming meek and terrified at certain points. Unsure of how to lead, of how to carry it all out. Still. On the floor, the bed, in a chair. Spent afterwards, they ordered a pizza.

More in the middle of the night, then some in the morning. She got up and fiddled with the cheap, small coffee machine. Brandon woke and saw her bending over looking through cupboards. Legs! He forgot everything just then. Every mistake he'd ever made washed down the bathroom sink. She passed him a cup of coffee.

Brandon took a detour to get Willamina to Des Moines. She opened the car door, and something shrank inside him. Another door closing. He had her name and address on the piece of paper she'd given him and watched her move out of view. Just a second, there she was, peering back and waving. He put his hand up and thought about the miles of asphalt that were still in front of him. To see her again in another incarnation. *I can make it on my own* in his head, then splintering. He pulled the car back on the highway. In not too long the Front Range would rise. A stopper. A curtain on his feelings.

He ordered a steak in a roadside restaurant in Nebraska. As he waited for the food to be prepared, he laid the three photos of Felix Welter down on the counter. Brandon realized that in the pictures, his father was close to the age he was now. *Look at the eyes, Brandon. Take in the profile in this one, the way he's standing. The way his head is slightly bent. A sign that life had given him a kick or two.* Back to the eyes and the jaw. He was looking down at himself. *I am him and he is me.* The inescapability. *Would I notice him on a sidewalk in some small town when he passed me by? Crossing paths with myself. Aren't you my son?* Brandon was done with the anger if there ever had been any. He knew no other life than that which he'd lived with Carrie Welter. And it was her he was attached to. It was his mother that he'd always look out for.

He went to a pay phone and called Abe.

"Almost there, Abe."

"Right on."

"Ten hours to Fort Collins."

"Rehearsing? Nervous?"

"Bit of both. I'm sure he's moved on anyway."

"The search not the find."

"Yep."

"I'll be in Spain in ten days. Then Eastwards."

"I envy you."

"Well, you've got this quest."

"Europe, Yale. You've got the world pinned to the ground."

"Maryland will be good."

"Close to Mom. That was the thinking. I met a hitchhiker. Turned out to be raucous."

"Female, I'm assuming."

"Yeah. She took me to school."

"To school? Or to the mat?" Brandon laughed.

"Have a good trip, Bubby."

Cornfields for miles. Radio. The path to God will open in front of you. You cannot hide from the power of the Lord. Click. Music. *And if they stare, just let them burn their eyes on your moving.* In the circle in his mind. Faith. I stand within, claim my belonging. Now, outside that circle. Still looking for guidance. To be pulled inside. Halt this lonesome wandering. To love and the bond, to my mother's health. He still prayed to St Dymphna, even if his mother had climbed out of the danger zone, for now. This beseeching always made him feel more self-assured. He would love and serve his saint to the end. Billboards. Long, slight upgrades, then coasting down. He checked the tires, filled oil, coolant. The air whistled in the windows. *I am here, nowhere else, traversing this land.*

Colorado. South, West again. Night. Coolie State Park. He grabbed his bag and set out into the woods. Fire. Food. Stars all around. Pitched the tent and waited for wild animals to circle. In the sleeping bag, arms behind his head. Tony Swanson on his mind, wishing him a safe trip, telling Brandon he hoped he'd find what he was looking for. Letting the Ashley thing go, no blame toward the boy. She's mine, but it doesn't feel like it, Tony had said, and now I've really got to let her go. And Brandon, listening to the birds making night calls. He thought of all those who had just one, or less. You can't make it if no one cares about you. So simple, yet so true. Ruminating about a vague future. Where he had come from, how much he had changed. The flab gone, in his mind too. Pulled his grades up, got into UM.

He woke, took a stroll through the stalks, past and under a lone willow tree. The river, bathing. Sun bursting onto the scene. Washing, eggs on the pan. Heat becoming oppressive. Where were his eyes? They were pinned to the nature, the splendor around him. The quiet. What will he be able to see? How much of it will he allow himself to take in? What of his nerves will disqualify this seeing? His mother on the floor. 911. The past is gone. No, use its essentials to aid you in the present. A cloud moves across, replaced by another. White, gray and black. In the tent now, he is devouring a book, as the sun beats against the nylon.

The car was making some funny noises just after he'd crossed into Colorado. He found a garage and pulled in. It would take a day. He planted himself on the local highway, bound for the nearest State Park, which according to his map was 35 miles away. He felt ridiculous for a second standing out there on the road ride begging. Pillows of ominous cloud were pushing in from the west. In a few minutes he'd be drenched. Otherwise, the sky was welcoming and boundless. He turned and looked back toward the East. Blue sky that wanted to lift Brandon off the ground. Twirling. Cupping his hands. He could find the path if he just set the right course.

    A man in a pickup pulled over to the side of the road in front of Brandon. He hoisted his sack and jogged toward the vehicle.

"Thank you, sir." The man waved his hand at Brandon casually. They drove in silence.

"Where to?"

"State Park, about 30 miles up the road."

"Skies are going to open up."

Brandon wondered at the man's slow way of doing things. As the first fat raindrops pelted the windscreen, and through the quiet, Brandon let his mind go. This man was the old Bubby Welter. The one who didn't care what happened to him. The one who would be pulled into anything against his will. *Maybe it was finding her on the floor that caused everything to start changing.* From dead to alive.

"Geez," he said. "It's coming down. Sure, you don't want some shelter tonight?"

"I'll be all right out there."

"I guess It'll pass."

Brandon had a few questions for the guy but decided to hold back. State Park. Brandon relished a night with rain pelting the tent. Hustled toward the shed in which a ranger stood. He bought a permit for three bucks and hurried into the wilderness. It was raining hard now. He didn't get far before he found a spot to pitch his tent. A game of getting it up as quickly as possible. Then he was inside, stripped down, toweling off. He got under the sleeping bag, which thankfully was still dry, and read the book by flashlight. What he couldn't understand in the book didn't bother him as much as it would have in the past. Willamina's tanned legs began to make the reading impossible. He put the book down and crossed his arms behind his head.

Carrie had her glitches and he had to forgive her for those. And all those hours being babysat by the TV. He was still trying to surgically extract the information from his brain. An endless stream of sitcom plots and storylines, the familiar settings, after seeing them over and over again. The irascible dispatcher, the grumpy detective, the hippie teacher, the sexy cruise director.

The plots of the shows made introspection impossible. All set up before you; neatly packaged stories force fed, shielding the complexity of the world outside the window. Assume that each and every form of human interaction will have a predictable stream, mirror the setup of the show. This scenario should match the one I just saw on TV. It will turn out in this way. And that brought him back to his father. They'd meet and embrace, exchange warm words, look each other squarely in the eye, take in the likenesses, geez it's been how long, embrace again, weep: roll credits.

Birds called out and the rain fell on the tent. Maybe a buffalo would appear out of the mist. The true owners of the land scattered in the distance. The book felt good in his hands. He flipped some pages, then ran his finger down the spine.

It's the search not the find. Tony too had had him practice getting into that arena where all thought shut down. It didn't entirely work for Brandon back then, but he was trying it now. The rain pattering on the tent helped. He took in all the sound and let it stifle his thought processes. A clear mind. It lasted about a minute and then his head and its contents were off to the races. The future occupied his thoughts. The large bowl of it with strange foods inside. Then the dishrag of the past, always squeezing. His mother. Her on the floor. 911. She zonked out in the ward. Then, a vague sense, once again, that he wouldn't make his mark, whether large or small, on the world. But mostly it was his mother. He wanted to get out of the tent and hustle to the nearest payphone to check in. He knew that would take some doing. He'd call her first thing in the morning. Brandon had to get over the sense that he'd let her down. That he was the one that sent her down the path she found herself on. He punched the top of the tent and the rain seemed to answer by producing harder and heavier drops.

The sun was out that next morning. It shone like a gift, and it was already warm in his hothouse. He got out of the tent and stretched, then went down to the creek and splashed cold water on his face and hair. He felt stronger and more prepared for what may come than he had in a while. Brandon dismantled the tent and packed up his gear, made for the road. He took a protein bar from his sack and ate it slowly, briefly prolonging the hunger that was going to rear up, that would be touched off by the meager nutrients of the bar. He waved to the Ranger and stood on the side of the road. No cars came by, so he started walking east. Eventually he was picked up by a man in a flatbed truck.

"Came down last night."

Brandon arranged himself on the seat bench. The man's words were slurred, and Brandon had a hard time deciphering them. "Excuse me?"

The man didn't look over. "Where to?"

These words, too, were hard to configure. Brandon stole a glance and saw the large scar running from the man's right eye down to the corner of his mouth. "I'm heading back to Adamsville to get my car from the garage. How far are you going?"

It took the man an eternity to answer. On the seat bench was a towel with an inch of an object poking out from underneath it. It may have been a tool, a socket wrench perhaps. "I can get you there."

"Great. I appreciate that."

The man started speaking in a monologue. Brandon had a hard time following him, and a strange anger spread through him. He seemed to be talking about his house and his rent and his troubles, throwing blame around. He picked out the words "fat cats." Brandon took another glance at the man. Then the truck went over a pothole and the towel on the seat bench moved. Brandon looked down and saw the pistol. All the anger turned to fear in a split second. *This is it*, he thought. Shot and thrown into a ditch. The man stopped talking and looked down at the towel. Get out. Stop the car, this is far enough. But Brandon was immobilized. He wasn't sure any of his bodily mechanisms would function. He had to get over it. Must speak. "Where do you live?"

The man's face was cold and blank. He looked over at Brandon. It took him a long time to do this. "Just up the road here." The man tucked the gun under the towel and set his eyes back on the road. He wasn't a large man, maybe 5'6, with a slight build and a potbelly.

"If it's out of your way I can… get out here." What it was like to get shot. The worst place for the bullet to enter. Brandon put his hand on his money belt. Driver's license, the prized cash, city boy written all over him. *He's slow. He wouldn't be able to get his hand on the gun before I made a move to stop him.* Brandon looked out his window at the scrubland. Those mountains he envisioned rising in the west were nowhere to be found.

"Settle down." These words came out in a crisper fashion than the previous ones the man had uttered.

A new stream of fear coursed through Brandon.

"Where you from?"

"Back east." I won't say anything else. I must talk my way out of it.

"Big city? All that?"

"No, I'm from a small town in Virginia."

"People living big out there, I reckon."

"Nah, you know."

The man stared down at Brandon's hiking boots. The gun peeked out of the towel again. *This is it. Where I come to my end.* The man looked over at Brandon and really took him in, did some calculations. It would be a struggle. *Should I go for the gun? Get him before he gets me?*

"Big city folk. Holding it over us."

Brandon had no idea how to respond. He thought of the bank statements of his mother's that he'd checked out those years ago. At least they were heading in the right direction, toward Adamsville. The fear lessened, then came on strong again.

"You work in one of those big buildings? All that?"

Brandon stared at the road. "I work on a farm."

The man looked over, less slowly this time. Brandon put his hand on his bag which lay between his legs. He saw the stop sign approaching. The man put his hand on the towel. Brandon fingered his money belt through his shirt. *Dumb move*, he told himself. Now, his hand was on the door handle. The man had his left hand on the steering wheel and his right hand on the towel.

"I'll bet you do."

Brandon wondered if he was going to speed up through the stop sign. He didn't though. As the truck slowed, Brandon opened the door and found himself standing on firm ground. He waited for the man to get out, gun in hand, for the bullets to start flying. He stood and watched the truck grind to a halt, then began to walk backwards in the direction in which they'd come. The man sat in the truck. Looked out the rear-view mirror. Brandon watched the truck make a U-turn. He gripped his bag tight and then slung it over his shoulders. Scrubland to the left and right of the road. When he saw the truck moving toward him, he took off into it. 30 feet into his planned escape, he tripped and tumbled to the ground. Then, he got up and began running away from the road. After a little while, he turned and looked behind him. The truck was parked on the road and the man was standing there with his arms crossed. Brandon ran for another minute, then stopped. *I could wrestle him to the ground. I could rip the gun from his hand before he shot me.* He had only the sky above him. Looking back, he could see that the man was not going to make any move to chase after him. It was a standoff. Brandon could read the desperation even from this distance. He planned to stay put until the truck pulled away. His senses returned and he could feel the hot sun beating down and his tongue was all puffy and dry from fear and thirst. Eventually the man got in the truck. He waited a few seconds and then pulled away.

Brandon spent a good part of the two-hour walk to Adamsville looking over his shoulder. Waiting for the man in the flatbed to pull up beside him, send a bullet into his body and haul off with all of his cash. He was a big city kid after all. His boots, even his shorts and the make of his T shirt said it all. It oozed off him. If it weren't for his physical stature, he'd be seen as an easy mark. Was flatbed man up for the risk? Brandon was sure he was. Head craned backwards again. He hugged the side of the road, walking through stalks from time to time just to get off the road.

He was sure the guy at the garage was screwing him. Brandon paid the bill and went across the street to get a meal. In the diner at a booth, he laid the three photos down. He was struck again. Amazing how much they resembled each other. It tore up his mind. Choices, leaving people behind. *Maybe it was for the best,* Brandon thought – although he knew no life than without his father – it could only have gone down the way it did. Maybe it would have been worse. And, why the quest? Brandon couldn't hide the fact from himself: he wanted to look him in the eye, yes, not to accuse him, but he also wanted to see this vast land. He had only been out of his city, for a long stay, several times. Trips to the Bay, horseback riding in the Cumberland Gap. Oh, and his Mother taking him in the hot rod to visit houses for sale in the Maryland suburbs.

The waitress who came over was chirpy. She tapped her pencil against her pad. "What'll it be hon?" Brandon ordered eggs and pancakes. "Coming up," she said. She took a few steps toward the kitchen, then stopped and returned. "Oh, get this," she said. "You just missed it. There was just a couple of coloreds in here."

What did she want him to say? "Well, that's an abomination?" Brandon felt static in his head and chest. She walked away. He looked out the window for people dressed in white cloth.

It felt good to be back behind the wheel of the car. He'd named it Brutus, and the reliable vehicle was holding up his end of the bargain. New state and the opening of possibilities. Colorado. He looked in the rear-view for the flatbed, concluding that that was all over now. The road unspooled in front of the car. They had given Carrie a diagnosis, but she didn't want to share it with her son. That sound of it alone didn't sit well with her. She wanted to go along as if it was just as normal, moving forward, taking things on as they arrived. It's like having heart trouble or

Diabetes, she had said. But the doubts and worries lodged in Brandon's thoughts.

The mountains appeared and had a calming effect. 1969 State Street. He pulled into Fort Collins and asked at a gas station where he could find the address. When he got there, he felt a tremor. This fear that made normal breathing difficult. It was an apartment complex, three stories. A For Rent sign out on the unevenly mowed grass. Brandon stared at the building, then he drove away. He was going to spend the night in the mountains and then return the next day.

He climbed up into the airy space, the town nestled below. Each step a form of renewal. Evergreens, and their scent, soothing his jagged thoughts and urging him on. This was the gift our land had given us. He pitched his tent and lit the Steno. A bag of noodles went into the pan. After the meal, he leaned back against a log and stared into the darkening sky, listened to the sounds of birds chirping, felt the wind lifting the small hairs on the back of his neck. UM was a big school. He'd made a commitment to be close to his mother and he would keep the promise. And he would have to find a way to better deal with people. Conform to society's pacts just enough.

The town was moving down there. College kids hungry, always on the lookout for excitement, for a fix. Right now, fix is these trees, this solitude, the escape into life. Brandon marveled at how far he'd come in such a short time. And time was on his side. He just couldn't throw his youth into the trash basket. The lights of Fort Collins. The feeling of entering something. The desire to talk to someone, the fear that that person will rob something from him when he went to speak. The hint of loneliness that infuses the solitude. He wouldn't let himself slip too far into himself. Not to go too deep so as to forget the outside world. He had the sudden urge to pack up and go down and enter a bar, just to make human connection. Two competing urges. Relieve the loneliness, pay the price of being engulfed by humanity. He got into his tent and picked up his novel. He could only read a paragraph or two. First thing tomorrow he would go back to State Street.

Chapter 15

What we are looking for may have been on our tail the whole time. Felix Welter had made the trip in reverse. He would show up on Que one day and announce himself. A knock on the door. Bubby Welter sluggishly walking to it, hands in his pockets, ready to be clubbed back a step or two. *He is me and I am him.* Come in. Have a cup of coffee, and talk about, what? We are mirrors.

1969 State Street. Quiet. A man mowing the lawn. Building in serious need of repair. Brutus parked out on the street, the feeling intruding: He isn't here. Brandon got out of the car and stood there for a minute or two. Then he found the super's office/closet on the side of the building. He opened the door and looked at Brandon with suspicious eyes. Another college kid moving in on his parents' dime. Brandon showed him the photos and a flare of recognition went off in the man.

"Yeah, I remember Welter. Worked construction. Didn't drink. Had a few girls come and go, but that obviously wasn't a problem." Something lit up in the man. Brandon smiled.

"Which apartment is he in?"

"Oh, he left about three years ago."

"Any forwarding address?"

"No. Although the day he moved out he mentioned heading west. Wait a minute. Yes. He had a lead on a job. Let me just think of the place." He scrunched up his brow. "Bay Area. But, not San Francisco. Damn." The man turned as if he could find the information in his work closet. "I'm sorry, son, that's all I can recollect." A light went on. "Santa Rosa! That's what he said."

"Okay. Thanks." Brandon held back, then spoke. "What was he like?"

The man glared. "He was quiet. Never caused trouble. Always had his rent in on time. Even pruned the hedges and shoveled the walk and didn't ask for anything in return."

He walked the streets. Behind every corner, Felix Welter was waiting, scoping out this kid who looked exactly like him. Eyes on the boy. Brandon kept looking over his shoulder, to the sides and straight ahead. He'd be able to pick him out in a second. There was nothing to say to him he now realized. *Why'd you leave? I'm so angry with you. Just picking up and leaving Mom the way you did.* He had none of those phrases at the ready and saying them would accomplish nothing. *Turn around*, he told himself. *Get on 80 East and prance back into the life you know.* Still, it nagged. He'd come this far.

Carrie was downcast when he called her from a payphone. He could hear the loneliness and desperation in her voice, even if she was skillfully trying to shield her son from them.

"I'm having no luck, Mom."

"Keep on."

He didn't want to ask this question. "How are you, Mom?"

I'm lost, Bubby. I see no point in going on. "I'm okay."

"Have you been to the Springs today?"

"I took a day off."

What to say: *Hang in there. Chin up.* It was all so trite. *I need to hustle back there. What if the past repeated itself?* "That's okay."

"Let go of your illusions, Bubby. That's what I'm trying to do." Silence. "I don't mean your dreams."

"Good advice, Mom."

"Fancy free."

"Get into the Springs tomorrow, maybe."

"I'm going to Brandy's this weekend."

"Oh, great."

A pause.

"Keep on until you feel you need to stop." The medication was what was making her speech so sluggish. It had to be that.

"Take care, Mom."

Brandon walked around the town. He saw well-dressed office workers, hippies, college students, pseudo-hippies, bookstores, coffee shops, expensive cars, jalopies, and vans. The air was dry, and the sun beat down. A fire could start up any minute. Around every corner lurked his father. He hadn't left town; he'd caught wind of his son's quest, and he was waiting to find him. Brandon bought a large sandwich, immediately felt guilty for its heft and the privilege of eating such a large quantity of food at once and took it to a park bench. If there was ever revolution in the air here, it had been subdued, smothered, and flattened out. The only remnant of that spirit was displayed in the style of dress and the shops selling Tie Dye clothes.

Brandon put on his running shoes and took off down the streets. A feeling of anger caught him off guard. Beating the pavement, shoes picking up and setting down gravel. After a while he hit that high. He ran through campus, looped around the football stadium, through a small commercial district and then back to the car. He checked into the youth hostel and got a bed in a communal room, wary of his money belt, sure he'd be robbed that evening, bound, and gagged. He aired out his tent on his top bunk bed. A pair of girls and a guy entered the room. They were ebullient and quickly enlisted Brandon in their conversation and doings. Brandon didn't let on about his quest; a plan was hatched. They'd meet back here at seven and commence.

Brandon lay on the bed. His sleep was fitful and filled with dreams as he looped in and out of consciousness. Being chased down the street by a huge broom, standing on the ledge of his high school roof waiting to be pushed or fall on his own volition, trying to shake hands with his father, yet when they went to do it, their hands turned to liquid, Mom on the floor, Grandpa taking the ultimate dive. He woke and looked around. A guy of about thirty was sitting on the bottom bunk of a bed. He had long hair and kept pulling it behind his ears, thinking? Brandon had the urge to speak, he had no interest in opening his mouth. He went out and bought a package of hotdogs at the grocery store and ate them on the steps of the hostel. The sun was on its way down and was losing some of its intensity.

    The guy's name was Len, and the two girls were Wendy and Kim. Len was of medium height and had long black hair. Wendy spoke more than Kim, who, though quiet, seemed less cautious and more apt to be willing to go along with things. They got in Brandon's car and Len directed them up into the Front Range. Brandon hadn't noticed it before, but as he looked into the rearview, he could see that Kim was holding a bag of oranges in her lap. Wendy spoke from expectation. She had a small case of water bottles. And Brandon saw his father on every corner, looking at him behind the wheel, sizing him up. Into the mountains. Onto a small dirt road that quickly ended.

    "On foot from here," Len said. "How long have you been

on the road?" The sun had gone down over the mountains and the temperature dipped accordingly.

"About two weeks."

"We've been going for a month."

"Where to after this?"

"Eastward, man."

"That's where I started."

They came to a small clearing and began collecting sticks. The fire came to life. Brandon threw wood and brush onto it, and it hissed and grew. Kim passed oranges around, and Len reached into his knapsack and produced the bag. The mushrooms were large, small, some of their stems stained a purplish blue. Brandon watched him lay them down on the grass, making four neat piles. Brandon had a slew of questions forming in his head but refrained from asking any of them.

"Psylocibin," Len said, grinning. "That's our captain."

Wendy clapped and then rubbed her hands together. Len portioned out the mushrooms and each of them went and took their allotment. The moon slipped free from a deck of clouds. The air had turned brisk, and a light wind prevailed. All of them nibbled at their portions, so Brandon did the same. He looked down at the town and tried to imagine what people were doing, how they were going about living their lives.

Kim dug into the bag of oranges and passed a second one on to the other three. Brandon poked a hole in his just to be able to start the pealing process. Then he brought the fruit up to his nose. It brought him into a delicious trance. He squeezed the orange, pealed it, had no desire to eat it. Len pulled out a harmonica and began blowing a tune they all knew. Wendy sang the words. Brandon looked up at the moon again. It was pink, then pale orange, a cotton candy white, its hue constantly changing. Then he felt a sudden urge and rose. Twenty feet away he bent over and emptied the contents of his stomach. The taste of the hot dogs he'd eaten and then a feeling of relief, a washed-out lightness. Next, Wendy's turn, then the other two.

"Got that over with," Wendy said.

Len put the harmonica down. Brandon stared into the fire. The flames licked the air, sucked in the oxygen. He couldn't take his eyes off it. Wendy removed her sweater. Len was making sure the other three were handling things okay. From the fire to the sky and then back again. Brandon saw the stars dangling, puppets on strings, the moon opening up and spraying the earth with love dust. He could reach up and become drenched in it. "How about a short walk?"

"My legs are all rubbery," Kim said.

"They look fine to me," Wendy said. Kim laughed.

They were up circling the fire, traversing the incline. Brandon was going to trip and fall down the side of the mountain. The feeling took over for a moment. For a second, he got scared. Deep into this notion that he'd never return to himself and his life. And then the thought: *so, what?* Kim put her hand out and Brandon took it. Energy passed between them, their skin hot and alive. He didn't want to let go. It was the most exuberant display of affection. They stayed this way until they got back to the fire. Wendy was holding Len's hand. The wind went right through Brandon's body. His toes were collecting messages through his boots. Any minute now, the sky would fall, and they'd be smothered. But, no, that was just a thought. Brandon's mind was a bowl with no bottom. No beginning and no end.

"Your hand is so warm," he said to Kim.

"Maybe because yours is so cold."

Len got up and put more wood on the fire. It crackled and

responded in the way that it knew how. Kim put her lips on Brandon's cheek and left them there for a sustained moment. It was the greatest thing that had ever happened to him. He touched her hair and said a prayer of thanks. Dymphna, the Lord himself. He had awakened from a deep sleep. Brandon and Kim lay down and looked up at the stars. It was so still. "We are lost in time and time is lost to us." Kim was smiling.

"Beautiful."

"What's a young-in doing out here all by himself?"

"I drove out here to find my father. He left when I was four."

She leaned back. It looked like she was trying to lick the stars.

"I don't know what I'm doing, really."

"You won't know, probably, until after."

They were quiet.

His legs were numb. He rubbed his nose to make sure it was still doing its job. "You might be right. I don't really know."

"Shooting star," Kim said. Brandon lifted himself up and noticed that Len and Wendy were gone. He looked alarmed. A brush of terror. The high was coming around in a negative way. The drug was digging in harder. He got up and circled the fire. The car, the hostel, the town.

"I'm going to look for them," Brandon said. Kim got up and touched his back.

"They'll be fine."

"This is starting to go bad."

Kim put her arms around him, and this eased things off. She whispered in his ear. "It's okay. Don't fight it. Clear your mind."

Easy for you to say.

Brandon found some brush and fed the fire, at once entranced by the flames. After a while, he began to feel calmer.

Standing there.

She could hear him thinking. She got up and gave him another hug. They stood like this for a while. The moon began to fall back into its rightful place, the stars too, the puppet strings cut. Dip, dodge, escape. His mind slid back into its old, rightful place. The lights shone from down below. The wind picked up and settled down. Len and Wendy had returned. Clouds swept by. A river moved silent in the distance, probably. They sat and watched the fire. Talk was slow, or nonexistent.

And before any of them knew it, the comedown began.

The next morning, after they had returned to the youth hostel, Brandon got in his car and drove over to State Street. He parked on the street and took out the photos of his father. Being thrown in the air, his father's arms pushing him up to the sky. Could this be a reliable memory? Was it just his imagining? The building was about to fall to the ground in a heap. Felix Welter was changing his diapers, gazing into the little boy's eyes. He was rolling a ball on the floor and little Bubby was groping for it. All a father's love one could imagine. Not a glance toward the future. Just the look into his son's eyes. He loved this little boy. But something happened. He couldn't sustain it, had no eye on the long game. Brandon looked intently at photos, rotating the thin stack of three.

His mother was mired in it. Her voice on the phone lacked energy. Brandon stayed on the line as long as he could, as long as she allowed. Where was that bubbly, if not crazed, person he remembered from the past? The one who flaunted and jerked. That was just a layer, a glitch, it wasn't her. Brandon forced himself to try and cheer her up, and by the end of the conversation she was indeed chippier.

He hung up the phone and looked around him. Cars went by, people out walking the streets. 911. The body on the floor. Brandon went to Dymphna, standing there in the phone booth. He even wondered if he could call her up. The phone book hung there on a chain. Was she listed?

Turning to leave the booth, a red sports car zoomed past him. There was no doubt it was Ashely Swanson behind the wheel still flicking the bird at life in general, and at him in particular, his wad of cash on the passenger seat. "What the...?" he said. The car rolled through the intersection and left his line of vision. She filled his mind for a moment. The fiery body sucking him into her plot. *Stupid, stupid,* he thought.

Brandon sat on his bunk and counted his money. Cash and traveler's checks. Enough for a trip out to Santa Rosa and back. August 25th he'd move into his dorm at Maryland.

They went to a club that night. Kim and Brandon danced. The songs went on for a long time and it was hard to distinguish when one ended and the next one started. Len passed a bone around. Wendy was flailing about and had fire in her eyes. The floor might have been dipping and bouncing up and down, the lights carrying their secret messages. Brandon put his arm around Kim. She kept dancing, lost in the rhythm.

Brandon went toward the back, looking for the bathroom. He entered a long corridor and just as soon as he did, the lights in that part of the club went out. He froze, and then began swirling his arms out in front of him. He kept moving forward. Other people were in the darkness. They were cackling. Brandon couldn't find the wall. He swept his arm to the side to find it, inched closer, but it wasn't there. All the light from the main part of the club was gone. Crept forward. No emergency exit signs. Nothing but pitch black. He stopped, found the wall, and leaned against it. Slid down and got into a crouch. But he couldn't stay in that position for long. He got up and started walking through the blackness. If only the door to the bathroom would present itself, then he would be back on solid ground. There was no bathroom though. Lost in the dark. He stopped moving and felt his body, maybe for the first time. He kneeled and put his hands on the sides of his head. Tremors in his fingers. A quickening of his pulse. No end to this in sight. He moved in the direction from which, he thought, he'd come. But it was only more darkness. He could follow the sound of the music. And this is what he tried to do. But he was only contained in even more darkness. *Well,* he thought, *I'll just have to accept the fact that I'm stuck.* The cloud in his head lifted. Still, the fear lurked. I'll lead you out. The words came from without, but they were clear. Just trust me and follow me. And then a click and the lights came back on. Brandon stood there transfixed for a moment. He looked down at his hands and sized up the movements of his fingers. Then he walked back toward the heat, the movement of bodies and the lights.

Chapter 16

Not far to Santa Rosa. Brandon had the windows down. Brutus had a lot of life in him. He spent the night before with Kim up in the hills, groping and wrestling with her. He felt wide open through the night, his voice unhindered, so they talked. Back at the youth hostel at five thirty. Heartfelt goodbyes with Kim – the exchange of phone numbers, the knowledge that passed between them that this was it, we'll never see each other again. He was going to spend the night in Nevada, then straight through to Santa Rosa. A full breakfast that last morning, then let Brutus take over. He could smell the border, then it'd be another five hours or so of road till he reached Santa Rosa.

The sun over the city that day he arrived was obscured by clouds, ominous grey clouds that almost came down and touched the ground, the river, Santa Rosa's winners and losers, those hustling toward their betterment, their cash out, others living on the fringes, still others stuck in holes they themselves hadn't necessarily dug for themselves.

There stands a man, scraggly brown hair and beard, clothes somewhat tattered, yet with a strange tinge, just a drop of newness to them, looking off into the distance. He had just emerged from underneath his tarpaulin. It was tied to a fence on one side and held down by rocks on the other. No one, not even the police, ripped this tarpaulin down. Each day, as the man made his rounds in town, he would return at night to find his tarp there where he left it. The river rolled southwards on the other side of the street. His bedroll was an old piece of foam. He carried it tied to his backpack when he made the rounds of the city. There were others in the row. The encampment. There was no time for talking now. The man crossed the street and washed his face and beard in the river with a small bottle of soap. He had found the bottle outside a convenience store one night. Some kind soul had misplaced it for him. The river ran. He swiped the soap through his hair and beard, and afterwards felt replenished. There was no need for deep thinking. He looked upstream and thought nothing. Just where to move to after this. More encampments along the riverside. Still more chances of being robbed. He thought, *Everything I own is on my person*. And the value of those things meant nothing to him. A book from the library, comb, scraggly toothbrush, toothpaste, foam mattress, the soap, the clothes I'm wearing. All they can take from me that which amounts to everything, is my body, and what's more, my soul. He was going to fight to maintain both of those entities.

He greeted George and Savannah who were emerging from their tarpaulin. Just a perfunctory raising of the head. Savannah had that deadened look in her eyes. The clouds were beginning to lift. It was going to be hot. The man walked north along the river, took a left and found himself standing in front of the kitchen. He sat with the others. The eggs tasted good. There was nothing to complain about. He looked around the table. No one spoke. Afterwards, he was pleased that he could relieve himself in the communal toilet. On his way out, Trisha, the woman who ran the kitchen, wished the man well with a smile that took her little effort.

He went up to the library and sat at a long table, immune to the stares. The newspaper on the wooden pole. He used to love waking up in Colorado Springs to the sound of the paper making that thwack on the front steps. In the stories, he could take a glimpse into the world he was living in, and one that was further away. Sitting at the table, his hands began to shake. This was something new. He squeezed them together, rubbed them against his thighs, becoming suddenly aware of how he looked to the people around him.

The newspaper held his attention for close to an hour. Then he braved his fear and took a run at the help wanted ads. Something in which he could use his hands. Masonry, carpentry, a construction site. He rubbed his beard. Something was off in his gut. Stares as he traversed the floor. A blemish, they all thought.

An hour later, crossing the street, he found a hubcap which was recently attached to an expensive car. He wondered how he could trade it in for some cash. He found a body shop. The guy looked him up and down. The hubcap was in pristine condition. twenty bucks. He went back to the encampment and sat on the bedroll. Savannah was screaming and George was trying to calm her down. An older man named Bell came by muttering under his breath. The sun burned through his tarp. He waited for his appetite to come around, then he got up and walked a few blocks to a diner. The waitress wanted to punch him, spit on him, or run away, or all of the three in that order. *You stink too,* he thought. She served him though. Half price on meatloaf. The man was presented with the food and made sure not to gorge himself on it. He pulled out his book from the bag he carried and thumbed through the pages of poetry. *About suffering* the poem started. He got lost in the words. The waitress was doing her best to ignore him.

Back at the encampment. This young guy was doing a herky

jerky dance. The man wanted to club him over the head. A police car rolled slowly by, and the man stared right into the driver's eyes. The car stopped and the two officers got out.

"Everything all right, here?" He was tanned and muscular.

No one said a thing.

"Any stuff coming through here?"

George pulled Savannah underneath his tarp.

"Keep it clean. We're always going to be here."

The man sat on his bedroll. They'll sweep all this aside. And then we're in the wind.

That night, the man went back to the kitchen and ate chicken and rice. It was the best food he'd ever tasted. He got up and sat on the front stoop of the place. Reggie, a woman that worked in the kitchen, came out and sat down next to the man.

"Why don't you think about coming here and helping out?"

The man looked into the distance. "I think I'll take you up on that."

That night, he couldn't sleep. He got up. Others were scoring and ingesting, but otherwise it was quiet. He went across to the river and watched the water moving. The river ran and it didn't question how it did that. He scooped some water up and splashed it on his face. Then he went back to the encampment. His legs were sore, and a tiredness crept into his bones. *Yes*, he thought, *tonight I will sleep*. Despite the disquiet, the movement, the night's activities, the jackals always on the prowl. *Time to block out*.

Brandon had taken the lower bunk in the common room of the youth hostel. There were four sets of bunk beds in the room and only two other beds were occupied. Before settling in, he went about town feeling listless from the heat and the scant amount of food he'd eaten that day. He had wanted to drive straight through from Nevada, and he was successful. Safe in his bunk bed, he reached into his sack and pulled out a box of crackers and some cheese. The cheese was soft from being in the heat, but he took out his knife and cut little pieces and placed them on the crackers. He ate hastily, not sure if he'd get enough. He began dreaming of steak dinners, pasta, baked potatoes stuffed with bacon and butter and sour cream.

The sun was going down when he hit the streets. It was difficult to find his way through town because he didn't know where he was going. *Sometimes*, he thought, *it was good not to have a destination in mind*. But, in this case an impatience impeded his thought processes. *Somewhere in this town lived my father, but I have no idea where he is or how to get to him.* If he was indeed in Santa Rosa. Night fell and the clouds released the view of the moon. Brandon walked the sidewalks. He became uneasy. Down by the river a small motorboat drifted in the waters. He felt it out of place. There should have been a barge or even a cargo ship chugging through the water. He crossed the street and set his eyes on the encampment. All the blue tarps lined up in a row. He immediately felt guilty about his car, the food he could buy and the clothes on his back. He got lost on the way back to the youth hostel and had to ask a couple of people for directions. The first man had said, "The youth are hostile. You can say that again." The second, a young woman in a red shawl, was more helpful.

On his bunk, he thumbed through a novel. Hunger ripped at him. He could always call and ask his mother to wire him some more money. But something held him back. One of the other men in the room struck up a conversation. He was going to hitch to the border and wend his way through Mexico. The cheese was sweating. This didn't stop him from spreading it over the remaining crackers. After, he lay back, protected by the bunk on top of him. He stared up at the coils that held the mattress in place. He was both inside and outside it at the same time. Accepted, welcomed in, then pushed out left to stare in with anticipation and anger. Forced to exist forever on the outskirts of the activity. Wandering. Only becoming more irate and more lost until he'd finally give up. The anger and ambition falling by the wayside. At what point would the circle open a crack to let him in?

He saw Dymphna clearly in his mind's eye. She had a flash of grace and selflessness in her eyes, and she was wiping Carrie Welter's brow. Carrie was at her submission. All the anguish was leaving his mother's body. She was set free purely from the kindness of Dymphna's sympathetic eyes and modest bearing. *Did Dymphna, though, ever look down on them?* Brandon brought the saint closer to him. He could reach out and touch her. He could become one with her. Why was she killed? By her father no less. The man deemed her a martyr. Or? That's when the third man in the room launched into a coughing fit. Breaking into his unwholesome cacophony. Brandon had seen him chain smoking outside earlier.

He put on a jacket and left the room. His money belt secured to his waist. In a convenience store, he got change for a five and walked over to a payphone across the street. How to find out her current state? How not to be overly concerned? How to comfort? Carrie picked up the phone on the second ring.

"Where are you, Bubby?"

"Santa Rosa."

A pause.

"Do you have enough?"

Brandon was perplexed.

"Enough?" She seemed on the verge of either sleep or tears.

"I do, I think."

When the child must parent the parent.

Brandon felt a strange anger rising. He clenched his fists and willed it away. *Are you out of your mind, Mom? Are you about to take another trip, another wild ride toward the ward?* A red car passed slowly by. Brandon was sure a drive-by would ensue, or that they'd knock over the convenience store. There could be pieces of him scattered on the pavement. *Must arm myself.* He rubbed his cheek with the mouthpiece of the phone. The car picked up speed and drove out of sight.

He couldn't bring himself to ask her a direct question about her health. Just having her speaking on the line had to be enough.

"Well, I should be back in a week or so."

"Wild goose chase?"

"I'm not going to find him."

A pause.

"Throw in the towel and get yourself home (to me)."

He was sure he heard her utter those last two words, but he couldn't be sure. Anyway, a spike of guilt drove through him. He became morosely quiet.

"Try again another time. But you won't find that lout."

Back in form.

"Come back to where you belong, Bubby."

My name's Brándon now, he wanted to fire at her.

"Yeah," he said.

"Just give it up."

He bit his knuckles. She was off on her voyage, and he wanted no seat on the vessel.

"Take care, Mom."

"You call me tomorrow."

"Sure."

"You're all I've got, Bub."

Another nail through his heart.

She was quiet finally. He said his goodbyes and with a heavy heart went back into the convenience store and bought a sandwich and a can of cola. He took these back to the hostel and at first didn't see his sack, then remembered that he'd stowed it under the bed, as if this would deter anyone from ripping it off. He laid out his clothes on the top bunk to get the mustiness out of them. Then, he lay down on his bunk. He was asleep in under a minute. Kim was in his dreams, beckoning him. Come with us, she was saying. It'll be all right. We need you with us. Circles. Of people, of trees, of chairs. Ashley and her demonic stare. Finally pushed to the edge of a cliff. How far down is it? Then waking with a gasp. He looked around the room to see if either of the other two occupants had woken or stirred. They hadn't. He looked into the darkness with a pervasive sense of dread and aloneness. His body said move but he just lay there basking in his loneliness. He tried to sink down deeper into himself but couldn't bat away the feeling of impending doom. Another dream would expunge the remnants of the one that came before.

He got up to a sitting position and nibbled at the sandwich. Stared into the slimy meat. The future traveler of Mexico tossed and turned, and his bed made creaking sounds. Brandon got up and went to the window. If only I could name all the trees I see out there. I'm sure most of them are palm trees. That would have to do. He spent a few minutes looking out onto the street below. It was empty of people. Not a soul around. Felix Welter was about to walk by. What would he be wearing? What would he be carrying?

That morning the wind picked up. Before dawn a newspaper page got caught in a gust and flew down the street spreading its news.

Brandon got up early and went by the encampment by the river. He passed some people, one guy with a scraggly brown beard and tangled hair. Others shuffling. The diner was nearly empty. Brandon felt queasy. He ordered tea, unready to order a large breakfast. The waitress was bubbly. It put him off. He ordered toast to go with the tea. He took out a pen and pad and wrote down the names of all the people he could call that day. Abe, Carrie, Brandy, Tony, Kim, Willamina too. The toast came. Dry. He nibbled at it. It didn't quell the queasy feeling that was creeping through him.

Outside. People are bathing in the river. I am torn by the money in the belt, the food that is readily available to me, the car, all of it. He was engulfed by a feeling of powerlessness and helplessness. He watched a man struggling to run a comb through his matted hair and beard. The sky reached upwards and outwards in a gulp of blue. The wind still had something to offer. He stood there and everything began to whirl about him, river, sky, trees, encampment, the stanchions that held up the bridge. When everything slowed, he noticed a woman in torn jeans, barefoot, coming across the street. She had nothing and everything in her eyes at once. "How 'bout some cash, mister? I seem to have fallen on hard times." Everything inside Brandon came to a standstill. He reached into his pocket and pulled out a one, passed it over to her. She looked at the bill, cursed and walked away.

An hour later, he was sitting in front of the LexisNexis cubby at the library. He put in Felix's full name. There was a fellow named Felix who ran a used car dealership. He had run afoul of the law, was in his seventies, and surely wasn't Brandon's father. He skimmed a few articles and then gave up. He sat there for some time and brooded. He was sure the man sitting across the way was the man he saw bathing in the river and combing his hair afterwards. The man looked up from the newspaper he was reading and stared out into space. I will never beg. For a moment, Brandon was sure the man had sized him up, studied him. Then his eyes settled on the printed pages again. He turned them over methodically. Brandon got up and walked the stacks. A flood of grammar school kids poured into the library. All the quiet dissipated.

Standing outside looking up at nothing. A fatigue came over the young man. Driven out of his life. That could happen in a flash. He too could be in that position one day. *Would I have the skills, the moxy to survive?* He looked at the building across the street. The distance from the ledge to the ground. Forever outside the circle. Who held the key to enter? *How did Grandpa do it?* Brandon shivered. He looked up at the building and felt himself on the edge of the roof. Sailing through the air. How dramatic would that be? Brandon wasn't a dramatic person, though. He hated scenes.

The man was stirring the soup in the large pot, hungry souls lined up at the long table. The right spices: yes, he remembered. He'd had a family once. A little boy and a wife. He couldn't avoid thinking about that time. He had come home one day, looked at it all, and found himself deflating. He was terrified of the responsibility and the intimacy. Then the great escape. To take it back. He ladled the soup into bowls and another guy brought them out to the people waiting hungrily. He'd thought about his son a lot during the intervening years and would fantasize about heading east to find him. In this state, there was no question that he'd do it. He would need to be presentable, had to have two feet on the ground, clean clothes on his back and his sense of dignity restored. And once they met, what words would be passed between them? There was so much in between the reality and what he imagined. So much distance, too much time. *Get through the days ahead of you*, he thought. Pull yourself up. You haven't lost it all.

Brandon put on shorts, T shirt and laced up his running shoes. As he left the city center, the houses started to get bigger, the lawns more manicured, the cars in the driveways primed for explosive motorized feats. The sidewalks held no cracks, the trees were pruned, the flowers lining the walks should have been exhibits in a botanical garden. He passed one house where a woman was holding a small child. She was giving him affectionate kisses on the forehead. The next house. A man was throwing a ball back and forth with a kid of about eight. Brandon turned and ran back toward the city center. He slowed to a walk when he passed the encampment. It wasn't far from the youth hostel. A police car was idling in front of the tarps. The woman who had asked him for money earlier in the day was being cuffed and led into the back of the cruiser. Brandon noticed that the woman was still barefoot. A man was pleading with the officers to go easy on her. Her worn feet were poking out the door. Brandon was caught off guard at the wealth of emotion rising in him.

He counted his remaining money. He went to the lobby and bought a sandwich and cup of coffee. He sat at a table and struck up a conversation with a young woman who was on her way to Berkeley to start school. She had thin arms and sparkling green eyes and spoke in jerky monologues. This didn't bother him.

Afterwards, he went to the payphone and dialed Abe's number.

His mother took the phone. "Bubby!"

He came on.

"Off to Spain tomorrow?" Brandon cracked a knuckle.

"That's correct."

Another knuckle. "Speak, Bub."

Wiggling his toes. "California is nice."

"Bub?"

"I've got nothing... left."

"Don't try and sell me that."

"I can't figure it..."

"Nothing to figure. Get yourself back here."

Another knuckle. Was it the same finger he'd already cracked?

"Yeah."

"I'll see you in August."

Toes going at it. "Sure, Abe. Have a good trip. Send me a postcard."

He was serving today. Bowls of soup passed around, sure not to spill any of it over the sides. Something grew in him, then faded. Dignity was built brick by brick, one right action after another. He went into the bathroom and studied his eyes. Looked deeply into them. *I am not my stench. It is only a layer. My dignity lies touchable right underneath it and it will push the smell away.* He pounded the sides of the sink. Then he went back to the table and ate his portion of food.

Brandon had an ache in his gut. He walked around with the three photos of his father. Who would recognize him? The pictures were taken over fifteen years before. He was too abashed to show them to anyone and he was becoming downhearted about the whole search. Afternoon came on, but the heat didn't relent. He found himself down by the encampment. The man with the scraggly beard and hair stood on the corner. Brandon slowed and the two stood face to face. Brandon reached in his pocket and pulled out a crumpled five.

"Keep your money."

"I, uh, just wanted to…"

The man stared right into Brandon's eyes. The wind picked up. Debris flew about in the air.

"Keep your charity for others, son."

A force whipped through the boy. The man still held his eyes. He was screwed into the street. Then the man turned and walked away.

Brandon got up late the next day filled with anxiety. His hands were shaking. He walked down to where the encampment, the tarps were. None of them stood there. It was an empty city block, devoid of people and their makeshift homes. He looked across at the river to find no one bathing or washing up. Keep your charity for others, son. The anxiety returned in full force. He wasn't sure he'd be able to put one foot in front of the other, to get anywhere at all. He did at last manage to propel himself forward. Once in the room, he packed up his belongings, found his car keys and checked out of the hostel. His feet barely functioned, and his head was whirling about. But move he did. Soon he would be on the highway.

In the car, he couldn't stop looking in the rearview mirror obsessively. His stomach lurched. He rolled down the window and thought of the tree outside their third-floor apartment. The natural, holy creation tapping, guiding, soothing. Groomed lawn, faithful walkway to the door of the building, Scott's, Abe, Tony, and his mother. He focused his eyes now on the road in front of him, the white lines, and the shoulder. It would be three days, come on you Brute, sleeping in the back at rest stops, gobbling food.

He saw a plane fly across his line of vision, climbing into light, through blue, heading for the outer reaches of the stratosphere, the sun making its sides glint. It could have been that ancient, human flyer from myth, heading out ambitiously despite himself, beyond his father, sure to be burned. Brandon pinned his eyes to the road again. Hands clasped firmly on the wheel, foot on the gas pedal, the sturdiness of the gearshift, America flying by on all sides.

His stomach had calmed, and the anxiety was gone. And as he urged his vehicle east, he couldn't help a smile from opening up on his face.